"I Want You, Erin.

And I want you to stay with me this morning if you will." All amusement vanished from his expression, replaced by so much desire that it took her breath.

Her heart thudded because she knew if she said no now and walked out, he would let her go. She had to make a choice here. All her life she had known what she wanted and didn't want. She knew now what she really wanted.

She didn't want to walk away from this man who had turned her world topsy-turvy, the first man in her life to set her heart pounding. The best-looking man she had ever known, as well as the most exciting. He was silent, waiting, letting her make her choice.

On tiptoe, she pulled his head down. With their lips almost touching, she whispered, "Someday, I may regret this moment, but right now it seems perfect."

Dear Reader,

Yes, we have what you're looking for at Silhouette Desire. This month, we bring you some of the most anticipated stories…and some of the most exciting new tales we have ever offered.

Yes, *New York Times* bestselling author Lisa Jackson is back with Randi McCafferty's story. You've been waiting to discover who fathered Randi's baby and who was out to kill her, and the incomparable Lisa Jackson answers all your questions and more in *Best-Kept Lies*. Yes, we have the next installment of DYNASTIES: THE DANFORTHS with Cathleen Galitz's *Cowboy Crescendo*. And you can be sure that wild Wyoming rancher Toby Danforth is just as hot as can be. Yes, there is finally another SECRETS! book from Barbara McCauley. She's back with *Miss Pruitt's Private Life*, a scandalous tale of passionate encounters and returning characters you've come to know and love.

Yes, Sara Orwig continues her compelling series STALLION PASS: TEXAS KNIGHTS with an outstanding tale of stranded strangers turned secret lovers, in *Standing Outside the Fire*. Yes, the fabulous Kathie DeNosky is back this month with a scintillating story about a woman desperate to have a *Baby at His Convenience*. And yes, Bronwyn Jameson is taking us down under as two passionate individuals square off in a battle that soon sweeps them *Beyond Control*.

Here's hoping you'll be saying "Yes, yes, yes" to Silhouette Desire all month…all summer…all year long!

Melissa Jeglinski

Melissa Jeglinski
Senior Editor
Silhouette Desire

Please address questions and book requests to:
Silhouette Reader Service
U.S.: 3010 Walden Ave., P.O. Box 1325, Buffalo, NY 14269
Canadian: P.O. Box 609, Fort Erie, Ont. L2A 5X3

STANDING OUTSIDE THE FIRE

SARA ORWIG

Silhouette® Desire

Published by Silhouette Books

America's Publisher of Contemporary Romance

SILHOUETTE BOOKS

ISBN 0-373-76594-0

STANDING OUTSIDE THE FIRE

Copyright © 2004 by Sara Orwig

This edition published by arrangement with Harlequin Books S.A.

® and TM are trademarks of Harlequin Books S.A., used under license.
Trademarks indicated with ® are registered in the United States Patent
and Trademark Office, the Canadian Trade Marks Office and in other
countries.

Visit Silhouette Books at www.eHarlequin.com

Printed in U.S.A.

Books by Sara Orwig

Silhouette Desire

Falcon's Lair #938
The Bride's Choice #1019
A Baby for Mommy #1060
Babes in Arms #1094
Her Torrid Temporary Marriage #1125
The Consummate Cowboy #1164
The Cowboy's Seductive Proposal #1192
World's Most Eligible Texan #1346
Cowboy's Secret Child #1368
The Playboy Meets His Match #1438
Cowboy's Special Woman #1449
*Do You Take This Enemy? #1476
*The Rancher, the Baby & the Nanny #1486
Entangled with a Texan #1547
†Shut Up and Kiss Me #1581
†Standing Outside the Fire #1594

Silhouette Intimate Moments

Hide in Plain Sight #679
Galahad in Blue Jeans #971
*One Tough Cowboy #1192
†Bring on the Night #1298

*Stallion Pass
†Stallion Pass: Texas Knights

SARA ORWIG

lives in Oklahoma. She has a patient husband who will take her on research trips anywhere from big cities to old forts. She is an avid collector of Western history books. With a master's degree in English, Sara has written historical romance, mainstream fiction and contemporary romance. Books are beloved treasures that take Sara to magical worlds, and she loves both reading and writing them.

One

"**H**ow did this happen to me?" Boone Devlin wondered for the hundredth time as he climbed out of his rental car.

It was an hour from midnight, the seventh of July, and the glistening asphalt parking lot of the swank San Antonio hotel was deserted. Boone strode across it, dodging puddles from the night's rain.

Summer lightning streaked through the sky and was gone, plunging the Texas night back into darkness. He walked briskly, still in shock over his inheritance of a nationally famous quarter horse ranch and over a million dollars. He was in town to meet the manager of the ranch and to break the news that he intended to sell it. He was interested only in funding his new air charter service. With the money from the sale of the ranch, he could foresee endless possibilities for his business.

The staccato click of heels caught Boone's attention, and he caught sight of a shapely female a few yards ahead who hurried toward the hotel. As his gaze ran appreciatively over her form, a man stepped out of the shadows and accosted her.

Boone couldn't hear the man's words, but she shook her head and snapped an emphatic no as she strode past him. The intruder fell into step beside her and continued speaking in a low voice. Abruptly, the woman veered away from him. When she did, the man reached out and grabbed her arm.

Clenching his fists, Boone sprinted toward them.

Already the woman had reacted, stomping her heel on the man's instep. Then, she slapped him hard over the ear and shoved him away.

"No!" she exclaimed again loudly, and while the man staggered, she rushed into the hotel.

Boone chuckled, and the man spun around. "What's so damn funny?" he snarled, starting toward Boone. The guy was ready to take out his anger on someone.

Boone clenched his fists and spread his feet. "You want some more?" he asked softly. He stood close enough now that he could face the man squarely.

Lightning flashed, and they stared at each other, eye to eye.

The man's chest expanded while he inhaled. Turning, he hurried away, disappearing into the shadows.

Boone sauntered into the hotel's elegant, deserted lobby that had leather chairs grouped around polished mahogany tables centered with vases of flowers. He strolled to the desk and checked in. When he went to the elevators, the woman from the parking lot was still there, and they entered the same elevator.

Boone had only seen her in the dark parking lot. Now, in the bright lights of the elevator, she stole his breath. His gaze skimmed over a figure that was usually found only in men's dreams. Her emerald-green sleeveless dress revealed lush curves and a tiny waist. Her slender arms had well-toned muscles, and he guessed that she worked out regularly. Especially since that display in the parking lot.

Her full red lips conjured up his curiosity about how they would taste and feel beneath his own. He glanced at her long, slender fingers and noted she wore no wedding ring. She was looking down, adjusting her purse strap. The thick curtain of silky shoulder-length red hair fell forward, hiding her face. She raised her head and he gazed into the greenest eyes he had ever seen.

Thickly lashed, her cat eyes mesmerized and enticed. They were cool, icy green, full of mystery and mischief and hints of sensual pleasure. She met his gaze with her own direct, self-assured stare.

"I was going to come to your rescue out there in the parking lot," Boone told her, "until I saw I wasn't needed."

"Thanks, anyway," she replied in a throaty voice.

"Would you like to go downstairs and have a drink?" he asked, hoping to prolong their time together.

She smiled briefly at him. "Thank you. Actually, I was going back downstairs. I haven't had dinner tonight so I'm going to eat not drink."

"Fine. I just got into town. Let me take you to dinner to celebrate."

Her eyebrow arched. "Celebrate what? Your getting into town?"

He grinned. "No, you fending off that guy. You were cool, collected and efficient. It was impressive."

"Thanks." The elevator doors opened. "Maybe I'll see you in the restaurant," she offered, and the doors closed behind her.

"Yes, you will," Boone replied quietly. He rode to his floor, hurried to his room to deposit his flight bag, wash up and comb his wavy brown hair.

Downstairs in the restaurant, he got a table beside a window that overlooked the deserted swimming pool. In the red-carpeted restaurant the lights were low and, because of the late hour, the room was almost deserted. While he sat and waited, he could hear live music from the lounge.

Less than five minutes later, she walked through the door, and his pulse skipped a beat. When he stood and waved to her, she hesitated, but then she smiled and crossed the room toward him, moving past the tables draped with white linen cloths.

He watched the easy sway of her hips, and his temperature rose another notch.

"You don't give up easily, either, do you?" she demanded.

"No, but I'm not going to coerce you into eating with me. You'll have to admit, it'll be far more entertaining than if we eat alone."

"And you don't lack in confidence," she added, sounding amused.

"That was fact not confidence. I know I'll have a better time eating with you instead of alone." He pulled out a chair.

"I don't usually let guys pick me up," she told him, "and I don't usually have dinner with strangers. For all I know, you're married."

"I'm not picking you up—this isn't a date," he said as she sat down. "And I've never been married, not married now, not going to be."

"A free spirit?"

"Exactly." He walked around to his chair to sit and face her. "Besides, we're not strangers now. We've known each other almost a whole half hour." He held out his hand. "I'm B—"

She shook her head. "No names. Let's keep this impersonal."

"You don't want to know my name?"

"No, because we won't see each other again after this night. When dinner is over we'll go our separate ways. I'll feel much better about it."

He cocked his head. "Want to make a bet? I'll bet you that before we part, you'll tell me your name. In the meantime, I'll just call you Red."

Smiling, she nodded while her green eyes twinkled. "All right, I'll take that bet. Winner gets what?"

"What would you like if you win?" he challenged, knowing what he would like to claim as his prize, but also knowing he couldn't tell her that now. Another loud clap of thunder boomed and crackled through the hotel. "What would you like if you win? Name something," he urged her.

She gazed past him and pursed her lips in thought. Boone had to fight the temptation to lean across the table and touch his lips to hers. Finally her gaze returned to him. "I'm a chocoholic. If I win, you get me a chocolate dessert, or if they don't have one, a candy bar. I know the gift shop will have them."

"Fine with me," he replied.

"Now, if you win, what do you want? You better keep the prize simple and impersonal," she warned in a no-nonsense tone.

"That you tell me four facts about yourself—in addition to the ones I figure out on my own."

He received another smile. "If you're trying to figure me out, I can save you the trouble. I'm an ordinary person who leads an ordinary life."

"I don't think so. Four new facts, right?"

"That's an easy one. All right. I'll take that bet and enjoy my chocolate."

"Tonight we can have a double celebration."

"This ought to be a good one—what else will we celebrate?" Outside, lightning flashed, and then was gone.

"My having dinner with one of the prettiest women in Texas, and that's saying a lot. Since Texas women are usually gorgeous."

She laughed and shook her head. "That's a little thick!"

"There! Your smile is absolute proof. You have a dimple, even, white teeth, a smile that would set any man's pulse racing, plus those big green eyes…" He paused when a waiter arrived to pour glasses of water for each of them.

Boone ordered white wine, yet all the time he was ordering, he was watching the woman and thinking about her. He had meant every word he'd said to her. Besides being capable and keeping a cool head in a scary situation, she was stunning and sexy—a combination to heat his blood to boiling. And he had the feeling that she was merely tolerating him. He could get some response from her, but it was slight and guarded, a rarity in his dealings with women.

As soon as the waiter left, Boone leaned forward. "Where was I? Big, green eyes, luscious red lips, fiery red hair," he said, catching a lock of her hair in his fingers. It was silky soft.

"Who were you telling all this to *last* night?" she asked, tugging her hair away from him. Though she was being flippant, there was no mistaking a chemistry sparking between them.

"I could deny telling anyone, but I don't think you'd believe me. The way you decked that guy in the parking lot says a lot about your personality."

"Am I supposed to ask you what you think my personality is like?" she asked with amusement in her eyes.

"I think you're practical. No frills. Intelligent and cool and confident. You're laughing at my compliments, which means you are self-assured and don't need to hear compliments. You can laugh at yourself and don't believe you are one of the most gorgeous women in Texas, though you should."

"Hardly! That's a real stretch." She laughed, and he wondered how many men had succumbed to that irresistible smile. "I've never won a beauty contest in my life."

"How many have you entered?" he countered.

"None," she admitted.

"And I'm right in my assessment otherwise—will you agree with that?"

Her lips firmed as she seemed to give his question thought before she nodded. "I'd say that I am practical and no frills. Intelligent—I hope reasonably so, but maybe I'm not showing a whole lot of sense eating dinner with a stranger. To my credit, when we finish dinner, I will go to my room and you will go to yours. And you won't accompany me to mine. You won't know which room it is. You won't even know who I am. Let's keep the evening impersonal. I'll feel safer that way. I carry a cell phone and can call for help at any time. As for cool and confident—most of the time. Not always. It's a fairly accurate assessment."

"So is the part about you being gorgeous." He leaned back as the waiter brought a bottle of wine, opened it and let Boone approve before pouring. The pale liquid half filled the glasses and then the white-coated waiter set the bottle in a bucket of ice and placed ornate red menus in front of each of them before he left.

As soon as they were alone, Boone lifted his glass. "Here's to you for handling a bad situation with great aplomb." He touched his glass to hers with a faint clink, and then gazing into her eyes, took a sip of his wine. The pale, dry wine went down smoothly while excitement hummed in him like an idling engine.

As she sipped and lowered her glass, thunder boomed.

"We may have just beaten the rain here," he observed.

"They've had two inches today already," she replied, looking outside and sounding as if she had forgotten him.

"How do you know that?" He was curious about her, wanting to know everything possible and wanting a date.

"The desk clerk told me."

While she talked, Boone caught her hand in his and felt a current zing over his nerves when he touched her. Her skin was soft and smooth. "I don't see an engagement or wedding ring."

"No, you don't," she replied with a faint smile. She looked outside again as if the matter held her attention more than Boone.

"And the way you said that, I suspect there is no steady boyfriend."

"You're right again. Maybe you should earn a living as a clairvoyant."

"I'm a good—guesser," he said, giving another innuendo to the last word, and she arched her eyebrows. "And another toast to a gorgeous redhead I'll always remember."

She moved her hand away as he touched her glass again. "Always being until the next pretty woman crosses your path."

"Not so. I'm not going to forget you and—" he leaned forward again and lowered his voice "—I hope before the night is over, I can see to it that you will always remember me."

She shook her head. "I don't think so, but you can tell yourself that I will. When we go our separate ways, dinner tonight will be a brief and soon forgotten interlude."

"I intend to see that it isn't," he said, intrigued more by her each minute. "So, I've given you a personality appraisal. Now, you give me one. I'm curious what you think about me and what you think I'm like."

"Self-centered," she answered lightly.

"Ouch! All I've talked about is you—where do you get this self-centered stuff?"

Her eyes twinkled. "You're aware of yourself. You're totally confident, determined, not a little arrogant, and in some ways, charming."

"I'm glad you threw in the last or I'd think I'd better get up and move to another table and stop imposing on you. 'In some ways, charming?' How so?"

"You know you're charming to females," she replied firmly. "You do not need compliments. You didn't get so self-confident by being turned down."

While she looked at the menu, Boone studied his. "How about the steaks?" he asked her, and she nodded.

"A steak sounds delicious. Actually, I missed lunch and had only a tiny breakfast this morning, so a steak would be wonderful."

In minutes the waiter returned and took their orders, leaving and coming back with a thick loaf of fresh bread on a wooden plank.

"You slice the bread," Boone suggested. "I'd mangle it."

He watched her slender fingers deftly cut two slices and offer him one.

He put a slice on his bread plate, but he was far more interested in talking to her than he was in eating. She had taken only a few sips of wine when he started to refill her glass.

"Thanks, I don't need more. Actually, I think this is the first wine—or any alcoholic drink—I've had—since Christmas."

"Christmas! Do you ever get out of the house?"

She laughed. "Yes, I get out of the house."

"Since Christmas, I think you can have a tiny refill," he said, looking at her questioningly.

She took a deep breath as she appeared to reconsider, and then she nodded. "I suppose. This has been a horrendous day."

"Uh-oh. I hope it took a definite turn for the better about half an hour ago." He refilled her glass and put the bottle in the ice bucket. "What happened that was so terrible?"

"I was at a business meeting," she said, and her voice became brisk as she stared past him. "Someone on the way to the meeting was in a terrible car crash and is in intensive care now and that put a damper on the day."

"That's tough. Sorry. Was it someone you knew?"

"Yes, but not well. And then my flight home today was delayed by storms, and we sat on the runway for three hours."

"You *have* had a bad day. Plus the guy in the parking lot. Well, the bad part is over, and I'll do my damnedest to cheer you up."

"You're doing a pretty super job of cheering me so far."

"I'm glad to hear that."

"Now I'm staying at this hotel since I couldn't go home tonight because of the storms," she said, sipping her wine.

"You don't have a northern accent. Hmm—where does the pretty lady live?"

"You're on a need-to-know basis tonight and that's another one of those things you don't need to know," she said, her dimple showing.

"Maybe," he said. She wore a delicate golden bracelet that was a chain on her right wrist. He touched it. "A gift from a boyfriend?"

"No. A gift from a friend."

He arched his eyebrow and looked at the necklace around her slender neck. An intricate emerald cross hung on a thick golden chain. "And the necklace?" he asked, leaning forward to pick it up, his knuckles lightly brushing her throat, but he felt the contact to his toes, and from the flicker in the depths of her green eyes, he suspected that she felt something, too.

"Is your necklace from the same friend?"

"No, it isn't. The cross is a family heirloom. Have you ever heard of Stallion Pass, Texas?"

"Yes, I have," Boone said in a noncommittal voice, keeping his expression bland, but inwardly he was startled because she was linked to Stallion Pass, Texas, so she must live somewhere in the area. The ranch he had inherited was near Stallion Pass. Maybe he could get this mystery woman to reveal her address.

"It's a small Texas town near here." He continued to turn the necklace in his hand, lightly brushing her throat with his knuckles. Each contact was electric, and he noticed that her voice had grown more breathless. He looked into her eyes and could feel the tension between them increase as the air sparked around them.

In a primitive, sexual way, she was responding to his light touches and his outrageous flirting.

"Do you know the legend of Stallion Pass?" she persisted.

"Something about a horse—I don't know the specifics," Boone said, remembering that his friend Jonah Whitewolf had received a white stallion when he got married. There was talk about the legend, but Boone hadn't paid close attention at the time because he had little interest in horses or legends.

"The name comes from an old legend," she explained, "where it was said that an Apache warrior fell in love with a U.S. cavalryman's daughter and persuaded her to run off and marry him. On the night the warrior was to come get her, he was killed by cavalrymen. His ghost was said to be a white stallion that forever roams these parts searching for his lost love. And according to legend, if anyone catches the stallion and tames him, that person will find true love."

"So that's where the town gets its name?" Boone asked, gazing steadily into her eyes while she talked. Once again, they were mere inches apart across the narrow table. He was only partially listening to her because the rest of his attention was heating in a fiery attraction that all but made the air crackle between them. As she talked, her words became more breathless and her voice lower. Her gaze never wavered from his. His only contact with her was his fist holding her necklace, yet the longing to kiss her was multiplying exponentially.

"Right," she replied, her words slowing. "There have been wild white stallions in these parts off and on through the years, so their presence has always fueled the legend."

He ran his fingers over the cross. "So where does this cross come in?"

"The maiden was brokenhearted to learn of her warrior's death. Instead of marrying a man selected by her father, she entered a convent. According to our family history, this was her necklace and it has been passed down through the years. We are supposed to be descended from her family. She had a brother who married and had children and the necklace was passed down in that manner."

"Giving credence—somewhat—to the old legend."

As she talked, he ran his fingers over the cross and felt an inscription on the back. He turned it over in his hand. And read, "Bryony." He looked up in question, rubbing her jaw lightly with his knuckles while he continued to hold the cross in his hand.

"So your name isn't Bryony?" he asked.

"No, it's not. Bryony was her name."

The waiter approached bearing their salads, and Boone leaned back, dropping her necklace and brushing his knuckles across her collarbone when he did so.

Over tossed green salads, Boone said, "You're a Texan and maybe you live in Austin."

When she gave him a mysterious smile, he knew he wasn't

going to get affirmation or denial. "You know this area if you're familiar with Stallion Pass and you couldn't get home because of storms. It's clear to the north because I flew in from there, but they've had storms moving through from west to east, so I'm guessing you must live in Austin and have to spend tonight here."

"And you're from…?" she asked.

"Near Kansas City," he replied, amused that she was trying to keep the conversation off herself. "I'll guess you work in television, in front of the cameras in some manner," he continued.

"You think so? This salad is delicious."

"Yes. If you were a singer or movie star or famous model, I'd recognize you. It must be television. You're far too pretty to be stuck back behind stacks of ledgers figuring out payrolls."

"That's ridiculous! You think I can't do that? You think there aren't some pretty bookkeepers out there?" she asked, her eyebrows arching while she sounded mildly indignant.

"There may be gorgeous bookkeepers out there, and I'm sure you could do whatever you set your mind to—I've already glimpsed you taking charge—I just don't think that's what you do. I think you're in television. An anchorwoman, weatherperson. You do some kind of show."

"You're not ever going to know," she said softly, leaning toward him with a twinkle in her eyes. "I will win our bet."

His pulse jumped again because she was giving him another challenge.

"We'll see. In the meantime, let's see what you will tell me about yourself. Brothers or sisters?"

"One sister who is divorced and lives in California and is a bookkeeper and is very pretty."

He grinned. "Okay, I walked into that one, but I said that

there could be pretty bookkeepers, I just don't think you're one. Will you tell me her name?"

"Mary. Plain and simple. She's an older sister. You're probably an only child or the only male with sisters."

"Why do you say that?"

"You look like a man accustomed to getting his way from early childhood. And especially getting his way with females."

"Why would you think I'd get my way with females in particular?" he persisted, enjoying flirting with her.

"You know full well the effect you have most of the time on females."

"Most of the time—that means this isn't one of them."

She shrugged, but the sparkle was still in her eyes, and he suspected she was enjoying the flirting more than she was willing to admit. "It's interesting to eat with you tonight, and I've had a long, tedious day," she said.

"Interesting. On a score of one to ten, I'd say 'interesting' is a five."

"Interesting is fun. And a five is good," she replied.

"Dang!" he exclaimed, mildly annoyed. "'Fun' and 'good' are not how I want to be known. Those are two bland descriptions if I ever heard any! I'll have to remedy the way the evening is going." A roll of thunder gave them both pause, and she looked out the window.

"Look at the rain!" she exclaimed. For the first time she sounded sincerely upset, and a slight frown creased her forehead. As rain drummed against the windows and water streamed down the glass in rivulets, Boone glanced at the swimming pool. Glittering bubbles popped up where raindrops hit.

"Sorry," he said. "You'll get home tomorrow morning, I'm sure. This will clear off and move on."

She bit her lower lip, and he stared, wanting to feel her full lips against his, wanting to kiss her. Her attention swung back to him and she blinked, and he guessed that briefly, she had forgotten him. Few times in his life had he had women forget, ignore or rebuff him, and the unique experience was both a challenge and exasperating.

The waiter brought their steaks and hot, baked potatoes sprinkled with chives. Then he uncorked a bottle of red wine that Boone had ordered to go with the steaks and filled new glasses.

As they cut into the juicy meat, thunder rattled the windows and another flash of lightning tore across the sky.

"We're getting a deluge," she said, sounding concerned.

"It'll pass and we're warm and cozy, enjoying delicious steaks and an unforgettable evening."

"It's going to be unforgettable, all right."

He reached over to take her hand, and her eyes flew wide as she looked at him.

"You can't do anything about the rain, and it will go away. No Noah's Ark needed here. Enjoy your dinner and let go of the worries. Let's have another toast." He released her hand and picked up his wineglass. "Here's to sunshine in the morning and excitement tonight."

She picked up her wine to sip. "I think I'm getting woozy from the wine."

"The steak dinner will take away the effects of the wine. Enjoy yourself and forget the cares of the day."

"I will." She took a bite of steak, closing her eyes as she chewed and he stared. She was one of the sexiest women he had ever known. He barely knew her—not even knowing her name, much less her phone number—and as far as she was concerned, she was going to walk out of his life and never see him again. He had no intention of letting that happen.

"This is the best steak I've had in a long time," she said. "I was famished. We had peanuts on the plane, but that doesn't do it when you've missed lunch, and breakfast was orange juice and coffee."

Another clap of thunder shook the panes and lightning flashed, giving a silvery brightness to the world outside. In seconds another brilliant flash crackled and then a loud bang came from outside. Inside the restaurant, the lights flickered and went off.

"Oh, my!" she said.

"It may be temporary," Boone stated, digging in his pocket and pulling out a small flashlight. At the same time, she removed a small flashlight from her purse and switched it on. They looked at each other and laughed as they placed the flashlights on the table.

"So we think alike on some things," Boone said. "We each carry flashlights for emergencies."

"Even if it's as dark as a cave, I'm eating this steak," she declared.

"So am I. Here comes our waiter."

The waiter approached with a candle in a hurricane glass and Boone noticed that other waiters were bringing out candles.

"This is just a temporary power outage," the waiter said as he moved glasses and set the candle in the center of the table. "A transformer has blown, and they hope to restore power soon. Can I get you anything else?"

"We're fine," Boone said, watching the white-coated man refill their wineglasses. If she was getting any kind of buzz from drinking her wine, it wasn't apparent to him. She was as guarded about her personal life as she had been when they sat down.

He touched the flashlights. "You're a practical person."

"Where were we when the storm interrupted the conversation?" she asked, once again moving the conversation away from herself.

"You said you thought I was an only child or had sisters. You're half-right," he replied. "I have sisters and brothers. There were nine of us."

"Wow! I'll bet you're the oldest."

"That's right and now I know better than to pursue why you think that," he replied. "If I guess your first name, would you tell me if I'm right?"

"Of course not! We have a bet that I would tell you, not that you'd guess. Remember? I want my chocolate bar. I'll take it up to my room and curl up in bed with it and read and listen to the rain," she said, sipping her red wine.

"I can think of some other things that would be more exciting to curl up in bed with than a chocolate bar and a book."

"I'm sure you can. You're not a big reader, then."

"I like to read. I just like other things to curl up in bed with."

"So what do you like to read?"

He named his favorite authors, and she nodded about some. As conversation shifted to books, he discovered how she spent a chunk of her time.

"Here comes our waiter again," she said.

"We expect to have electricity soon," the white-coated man said when he paused at their table. He had a sack in his hand and produced a bottle of white wine. "Compliments of the house. We're sorry for any inconvenience tonight because of the lights."

"Thanks," Boone said when the waiter returned the bottle into the sack and set it on the table.

When they finished eating, Boone had the dinners put on his room bill in spite of her protests. They talked about books a few more minutes until he took her hand. "Let's go to the lounge. I can hear music, and we can dance."

She inhaled and he saw a flicker of eagerness in her eyes and he knew she was debating whether or not to accept his offer. Still holding her hand, he stood and pushed away his chair. "C'mon, mystery lady. A few dances will be a pleasure. You're safe with me."

"I think you're the biggest danger I've encountered in a long, long time," she said softly.

Two

"That's progress," her handsome escort replied. "Knowing I'm dangerous to you just moved me out of 'fun' and 'good' for the evening."

Knowing she should say no yet unable to resist, Erin picked up her flashlight and purse and handed him his flashlight. When her fingers brushed his, she drew a sharp breath. The slightest contact with him tonight had been electric. He was irresistible and he knew it and she was certain he had left an abundance of broken hearts strewn in his past. With all her being she was trying to keep a wall between them because there was a volatile chemistry that had sparked to life the first moment she had looked into his blue eyes in the hotel elevator.

He was so incredibly handsome! All evening it had been an effort to keep from staring at him.

In the dark lounge, he led her to a corner table. The place was half filled and a few couples circled the dance floor. Two walls were dark paneling with hunting pictures, mirrors

backed the bar and the fourth wall was French doors opening to a terrace. Each table had a candle, and the entire bar
was in semidarkness, yet with the candlelight, the room held
a cozy atmosphere.

She watched while her new acquaintance ordered glasses
of white wine. Golden candlelight flickered over his well-
shaped hands. Her gaze drifted up. The yellow candlelight
highlighted his prominent cheekbones and threw the hollows
of his cheeks into shadows. His sexy, thickly lashed bedroom
eyes guaranteed easy conquests and his full lower lip hinted
at sensuality.

When she looked at his thick, wavy brown hair that was
neatly trimmed above the strong column of his neck, she
knew she was openly staring, but he was the handsomest man
she had ever known. Only she didn't really know him and she
was wary of his flirting. All her life the only men she had
dated were men she had known as friends. She never had
blind dates, had never had a flash encounter that resulted in
something more.

A short-sleeved navy sport shirt revealed this man's impressive muscles that indicated he either worked out daily or
was into a job that took a lot of physical labor.

She already knew his broad shoulders tapered to a narrow
waist and trim hips. The sexy, charismatic man was danger-
ously appealing.

Unaccustomed to alcohol in any degree, she knew she
should stop drinking wine, because she needed her wits to
deal with such a heady combination of male sexuality and
charm. And she suspected he was intent on seduction.

Her day had been dreadful. When she had flown into town,
she had been exhausted and hungry only to be accosted in the
hotel parking lot, adding to the miserable day. Encountering
her dinner companion in the elevator with his cocky charm

had made her smile and relax. All his talk about how gorgeous she was—she was certain he heaped the same compliments on any woman he dated. Still it was nice to be the object of those compliments.

She had wanted to get off the elevator and forget about him, but the man was too handsome to easily erase from memory. And in the elevator there had been sparks of attraction between them. She had felt it and she knew he did, but then, he probably experienced sparks with most of the females he encountered.

The moment she had stepped into the restaurant and spotted him across the room, her pulse had leaped.

Maybe it was the wine, but she felt exhilarated. All her tiredness and worries of the day had evaporated, and she had appeased hunger with a delicious steak dinner.

He stood and held out his hand. "Let's dance."

Taking his hand, tingles sizzling from that impersonal contact, she went with him to the dance floor, stepping into his arms and onto dangerous ground. Now she was in his arms, and every nerve in her body quivered. She could detect a tangy aftershave. Her thighs brushed his thighs. She was held lightly against him and she could feel the warmth of his body.

Giddy and breathless, she told herself it was the effects of the wine, but she knew it wasn't. It was the man.

Dancing was paradise, and her partner was fascinating. How long since she had danced? She couldn't remember. Probably last Christmas's barn dance at the Kellogg ranch.

His arm tightened slightly, pulling her closer. They danced together with an ease that surprised her. At five-eight, she usually didn't have to look up to men she was with, but she did now. He was well over six feet tall.

The next song was a fast number, and he swung into it without asking her. She danced around him, caught in the intensity of his blue-eyed gaze, knowing she enticed him just as he excited her. He caught her and spun her around, leaning over her, and for an instant they were frozen as she clung to him and gazed up into his eyes and saw the longing in their depths.

He swung her up, and they finished the dance and then began a slow dance.

"My head is spinning."

"It'll stop spinning with this music. Now it's slow, deliberate, languid," he drawled softly, his breath fanning her hair as he pulled her close and wrapped his arms around her.

She should push against him and step back to keep the dancing as impersonal as possible, but it was heaven to be held in his arms. She closed her eyes to enjoy herself without reservation. She was dancing with the most handsome, appealing man she had ever known. And the sexiest. She didn't even know his name and they would soon part and never see each other again, but right now she was going to dance and enjoy another hour with him.

How long since she had been on a date and had experienced as much excitement? She knew the answer had to be calculated in years, not days or months. Which made her all the more vulnerable to the man's magnetism.

He wanted to know her name, and instinctively she realized for her own well-being, she should keep a barrier between them. The wine had been a mistake because she knew her judgment had slipped or she wouldn't be here, wrapped in his arms, slow dancing with him.

His arms tightened just a fraction, and they were barely moving now.

Why couldn't one of the locals who wanted to date her have been like this? Excitement bubbled in her, and she kept telling herself to be careful, to resist this charmer whose name she didn't know.

"I've thought of a list of names that might fit you—Laura, Emily, Katherine, Kate, Patricia," he whispered, his warm breath tickling her ear.

"None of the above," she answered, leaning away to look up at him. The moment their gazes locked, her heart thudded. He wanted her and he wasn't hiding it.

"I'll tell you *my* name," he said quietly, and she put her fingers against his mouth to stop him.

"Don't tell me," she whispered, intending to be emphatic, but her voice wavered as he kissed her fingers. Her stomach clutched and desire became a low flame inside her.

She sucked in her breath. "No names—remember?"

"I remember and I intend to win our bet." He took her hand in his again and pulled her close and they danced. She moved with him, her fingers on his shoulder.

"I intend to figure out your name and to take you out again," he declared.

While her pulse skittered, she leaned away to look up at him. "You don't know where I live."

"The world is a small place, and I get around a lot."

"I'll bet you do."

"And for you, a man would be willing to go to the ends of the earth."

"For a date? I don't think so."

He danced to the French doors and opened a door. Outside on the terrace, water ran from downspouts and dripped from the eaves, but the rain had stopped.

"Where are you going?" she asked as cool, damp air enveloped her. When they danced through the door onto the terrace, she felt a light mist.

"Out here where we can be alone," he said, still dancing with her and closing the door behind them. He waltzed into the shadows.

"I think we're getting rained on," she remarked.

"Have you ever been kissed in the rain?"

Her heart pounded as she shook her head. "No, I haven't." She met his gaze squarely. She should look away, move away, do a thousand other things besides stand in his arms, but his compelling eyes held her. When his gaze lowered to her mouth, she couldn't get her breath.

His hand tangled in her hair while his arm tightened around her waist, pulling her closer against him. When he lowered his head, she closed her eyes, wrapping her arm around his neck and turning her mouth up to his.

His tongue touched hers, and then he kissed her deeply. She was hopelessly lost as he leaned over her. Standing on tiptoe and kissing him in return, she wrapped both arms around his neck.

Her heart thudded, drowning out all other sounds. Her world narrowed to his kiss, sensations streaking in her and building a heat low in her body. Stunned by passion and the stormy longing that swamped her, she moved her hips against him and felt his arousal press against her.

A fiery hunger raged, and she ran her fingers over his strong shoulders and slid her hands up to tangle her fingers in his thick hair. Never once in her life had she been swept beyond reason into passion as she was this night.

Lights exploded behind her closed eyelids while she was consumed by longing. What was probably nothing unusual to him was a once-in-a-lifetime happening with her.

His tongue stroked hers, fanning the flames already blazing. Suddenly he leaned away a fraction. With an effort she opened her eyes, and her heart missed beats. His blue eyes blazed with desire until she felt as if she could be devoured merely by a look.

"Who are you, darlin'? I want to know you. What's your name?"

"Erin," she replied breathlessly, knowing she was crossing a line. "What's yours?"

"Boone Devlin," he answered, leaning down to kiss her again.

As shocked as if ice water had been poured over her, Erin pushed against his chest and stared at him. "Boone Devlin!" she exclaimed.

"You act like you know me," Boone said, not caring at the moment and tightening his arm around her waist while she pushed harder against his chest.

"You're Boone Devlin!" she exclaimed again, her eyes widening while she stared at him as if he had just sprouted purple hair.

This time her amazement got through to him and Boone leaned away, frowning. "Yes, I am. Do we know each other? I don't think we do," he replied as fast as he asked the question. "I couldn't have possibly forgotten meeting you."

"No, we don't know each other, but we're going to. I'm Erin Frye."

"Damn!" he breathed, in turn shocked to learn her identity. "Erin Frye, the manager of the Double T Ranch?" he asked as he stared at her.

She nodded. "You know, we're getting wet out here, and the mist is thickening. Let's talk inside."

Stunned, Boone could only gape at her while all his preconceived notions and imaginings of a tough, older ranch woman shattered into oblivion. "You run the ranch?"

She nodded and held her hand palm upward to feel the rain. "It's *wet* out here, Boone."

He was totally stunned because she was absolutely nothing like he had imagined the manager of his ranch to be. The words the attorney had used to describe her spun through his memory: competent, tough, capable, experienced at ranching, knows horses, reliable, trustworthy. There hadn't been one word about beauty, or being alluring or exciting.

"If you want to stand in the rain, you go ahead," Erin said briskly. "I'm getting wet and I'm going in." Turning, she headed into the hotel, and he came to his senses and caught up with her, taking her arm.

"Let's adjourn to my suite and have coffee sent up and talk about this," he said.

As she turned to look at him, he was certain that she was going to say no. "C'mon, Erin. We're going to have to work together at the Double T, after all," he urged.

She blinked as if she had never thought of such a possibility and then she nodded.

"Great," he said, and motioned to a waiter. In minutes they were in the elevator, and Boone had the corked, complimentary bottle of wine in hand.

"I thought you were going to get coffee," she said, eyeing the wine bottle. "I've had more wine tonight than I've had in the past two years."

"We need to celebrate again," he said, moving close, sliding his arm around her waist. He wanted her more than he could remember ever wanting a woman before. "Erin Frye," he said in a low voice, and she took a deep breath as her eyelids fluttered.

"I still can't believe that *you're* Boone Devlin," she whispered. She sounded breathless, and he could see desire in the depths of her green eyes. He leaned down to kiss her, wrapping his arms around her tightly.

Erin turned her face up to his. Now he wasn't a stranger. She knew some of his history. And it was impressive. His years in Special Forces and his daring rescue of John Frates. John Frates had spent hours telling her about the men who'd saved him and how special and capable and brave and intelligent they were. For over the past four years she had been hearing about Boone Devlin, so the man was no stranger. And her caution and resistance crumbled into nothing.

Oblivious of her surroundings, Erin returned his embrace, kissing him while her heart pounded and passion possessed her. Wanting his kisses with an urgency that shook her, she poured her desire into her kisses. She was dimly aware when he walked her backward out of the elevator while he continued to kiss her. She pushed away and looked around the empty hall. "Where are we?"

"Almost to my room," he said. He took her arm and led her down the hall. Her head was spinning, she was breathless, hot, and wanting to be back in his arms.

He unlocked a door, pushed it open and led her inside, kicking the door shut behind him and pulling her into his arms while he set the wine on a nearby table.

As they kissed, he leaned back against the door. His hand slid over her, stroking her back, sliding down over her bottom and her hips.

She trembled with desire. Holding him, she wanted him desperately. She kissed him, pouring pent-up needs and brand-new longings into her kisses. Unfastening the buttons of his shirt, she caressed his bare chest, tangling her fingers in a thick mat of hair.

He made a growling sound deep in his throat, and she could feel his heart pounding. When he shrugged off his shirt and dropped it, her desire ratcheted another notch. His sculpted chest was muscled, tapering down to a washboard stomach, and the word *awesome* came into her mind.

While she was consumed by passion, she could see the effect she was having on him. From the first moment, knowing him had been magical. Now to discover he was someone she had been hearing about for years was like being with someone she had known a long time.

As she ran her fingers across his chest, she was only dimly aware of his fingers at the zipper of her dress. In seconds it was gone, falling to the floor with a swish around her ankles. Pushing away her lacy bra, his fingers caressed her breasts, and she moaned, shaking and overcome by his seductive caresses.

"Ah, Erin, you're beautiful!" he whispered, bending down to take her nipple in his mouth. His tongue circled the taut bud while she tangled her fingers in his hair with one hand and tugged at his belt with the other.

His hands brushed hers and then his trousers fell around his ankles. He kicked off his shoes, peeled away his socks and stepped out of his trousers. He leaned away, discarding his shoes and socks while she ran her hands over his magnificent body.

The man was all hard muscle. She leaned forward to shower kisses over his chest and heard him inhale deeply.

Her head spun and she was on fire. While he kissed her, he picked her up in his arms and carried her to his bed. He put her on the mattress and moved over her to trail kisses on her breasts, to stroke and kiss her nipples, first one and then the other, and then he traced kisses lower. His hands caressed her legs, sliding between her thighs and touching her intimately.

Erin was drowning in his lovemaking, her pulse drumming out all other sounds, her closed eyelids shutting out awareness of anything except his hands and mouth on her. She tangled her fingers in his hair and wanted him with a need she had never known in her life.

His slightest caress and kiss drove her wild. While her head thrashed back and forth, she moaned softly, stroking him, wanting to give herself to him completely. He was incredibly special and what had happened between them was unique, something she never thought would happen.

Was she starry-eyed? In a dreamworld of fantasies? she asked herself. She didn't care as she ran her hands over his strong shoulders. She glanced at him to see him leaning over her, his taut muscles taking her breath, and she closed her eyes again.

She clung to him as if he were the only solid thing in a world spinning crazily away. And even though they had just met for the first time tonight, he was no stranger. She knew myriad details about his past life. Knew what foods he liked and didn't like, where he lived. She had seen pictures of him, but she hadn't connected the pictures with the man because they had been photos taken at a distance, blurred, worn with time. They were pictures of a shaggy-haired man with a cap on. The cap was gone and the long shaggy hair was gone and he didn't look as thin as he had in the pictures.

Boone wanted her with a hunger that was amazing, and she wanted him with a need that was staggering.

He touched her intimately, stroking her, driving her to oblivion, and then his tongue was on her, heightening all the need he had already built in her.

"Boone, please…" She whispered his name, her words fading away. She gasped, sitting up and wrapping her arms around his neck to pull him down while she kissed him. Then she took his shaft and slowly kissed him, feeling him tremble until he came up off the bed to wrap his arms around her so tightly it took her breath. He cradled her against his shoulder, kissing her and making her tremble.

"Love me. Love me now. This will be a night to remember."

He leaned over her, laying her down on the bed again while he knelt between her legs.

"Are you protected, Erin?"

She shook her head and he stepped off the bed. When he did, she sat up and caught his arm. "Boone—"

"Just a minute," he said, crossing the room to retrieve a packet from his flight bag. He returned and leaned over her to take her in his arms and kiss her.

When he moved between her legs, she stared at him, memorizing each detail about him while her heart pounded with eagerness. When she looked into his eyes, her breath caught.

Blatant desire burned in blue flames. She held out her arms and he came down into her embrace and then so slowly entered her.

"Boone! I want you!" she cried out, wrapping her long legs around him tightly.

"Ah, Erin, darlin'." He moved slowly and withdrew and she gasped, arching against him and pulling him to her as he entered her again slowly and then he halted. "Erin!"

"Love me," she whispered, pulling at his shoulders. He raised up slightly, startling her. She opened her eyes to look up at him and see a frown creasing his forehead.

"You're a virgin!" When he started to scoot away, she held him, her arms tightening.

"Make love to me, now, Boone. I want you," she cried fiercely, tugging him to her. She leaned up to kiss him, catching his lower lip gently in her teeth and then stroking his lips with her tongue before her tongue went into his mouth.

"Erin, you don't know—"

"Yes, I do know!" she exclaimed. "I want you!" She pulled him down, kissing him as she held him tightly with her arms around his neck.

He entered her again and she felt the tightness, some pain, and she knew he was about to pull away again, but she clung to him. He entered her fully, filling her slowly, and in seconds urgency drove her to a wild rhythm with him.

"Boone!" she cried in a frenzy.

"Erin, darlin'." He kissed her while they moved together,

and then they crashed over a brink and stars exploded behind her closed eyelids as ecstasy enveloped her.

They gradually slowed, their pounding hearts returning to normal, their ragged breathing leveling out.

He kissed her and stroked her and finally rolled onto his side, keeping her with him. She opened her eyes to find him watching her.

"Boone, I think I'm in heaven."

He tightened his arms around her and smiled at her before he pulled her close and kissed her gently. "You're beautiful and wonderful and I can't believe my fortune," he whispered. He framed her face with his hand. "You were a virgin. I know I must have hurt you."

"Not really," she told him, caressing his cheek, feeling the short stubble.

Erin was still euphoric from their lovemaking.

He stroked her back while he showered her with light kisses, kissing her temple, her cheek, her throat. He brushed her tangled hair away from her face. "I want to hold you forever," he whispered.

"I still can't believe it's you. I've heard about you for over four years now and I knew you were coming to the ranch sometime soon, but I didn't know exactly when."

"I called and left messages."

"I haven't been there to get them."

She stroked his shoulder and his marvelous chest, leaning away slightly to look at him while she ran her fingers over his jaw, then down again across his chest.

"So you flew into town tonight?" she asked.

"This afternoon. I was with my friends the Remingtons and Whitewolfs."

"I've heard about them. And I've met Mike Remington. They were in the military with you and were included in John's will."

"That's right."

"If you were with them in the afternoon—you already had dinner when you ate again with me."

He grinned. "I wanted to eat with you."

She rubbed his flat stomach. "Can't tell you've had two dinners."

"I've worked it off," he said, and she smiled. "The Remingtons wanted me to stay with them tonight, but I came back to the hotel."

"I'm glad. This never would have happened if you had stayed at their house. Or if it hadn't rained, because I would have flown into town and gotten my car and driven home, but that's why I'm in the hotel. Earlier tonight they had a gully washer and a bridge to the ranch is out."

"I would have come to Texas sooner if I had known about you."

She smiled at him as she stroked her hand over his hip and down his thigh. Something flickered in the depths of his eyes and he rolled away to stand, picking her up in his arms.

He carried her to the shower where he set her on her feet and turned on the water, watching her all the time. They soaped each other off, slowly, their gazes locked, and desire flared again in Erin and she knew he wanted her. He was hard, his shaft thick, ready for loving. She wound her arms around his neck and stood on tiptoe to kiss him.

He turned off the water and grabbed towels and they toweled each other dry and in minutes were kissing again. He carried her back to bed to pull her into his arms.

"I don't want to hurt you anymore tonight. We'll wait, darlin'. We can kiss and cuddle for now."

"I didn't know it could be like that," she said as she snuggled into his embrace. He ran his fingers up and down her back.

"It can get better than this for you. Long, slow, loving, and it'll be the best ever."

As he held her with his fingers lightly tangled in her hair, he asked, "How did you get to be manager of the ranch? You're young for that job."

"Not so young. I've grown up around ranch work all my life." She lay wrapped against him, her legs entangled with his, the sheet under her arms, and she gazed into his blue eyes. Bubbly, excited, she wanted to talk to him, to touch him, to kiss him. It was an effort to pay attention to his conversation, and she fought the temptation to pull him close and kiss him again. His fingers moved over her shoulder and down her arm, tingles dancing in their wake.

"I inherited my job," she replied breathlessly. His light strokes that were casual were stirring desire. "My father was the manager, but he had poor health. My mother died when I was young."

"I lost my dad when I was young—I was eleven," Boone said. "How old were you when your mom died?"

"Fourteen and my sister, Mary, was sixteen."

"It's rough, but you survive because you have to."

"Through the years my dad taught me how to do the things he did, so when I had to take over, it was gradual and I knew what I was doing."

"And you like your work?"

"I love it. That ranch is my whole life. My family has worked for the Frates through generations—since the first Frates settled on the land." She touched Boone's chin lightly, gazing up at him. "Are you coming down here to try to make a lot of changes?"

"Right now, I want to see the place and how it works. You can help me with that."

Her heart skipped a beat as she gazed up at him.

He kissed her lightly on the temple. "You're not at all what I imagined. I'm still amazed."

"John thought the world of you and the other guys who rescued him," she said.

"I'm still in shock over my inheritance. All three of us were stunned to learn we inherited fortunes from John Frates."

"You saved his life when he was held hostage," she said while Boone toyed with locks of her hair. She felt the faint tugs against her scalp.

"That was our job in Special Forces. We were just doing what we were supposed to do," he said. "That's the way all of us feel about it."

"There were four of you, weren't there?"

"Yes," Boone said, his eyes getting a faraway look. "Colin Garrick. He was killed in another operation later. An exceptional man."

"I'm sure all of you were exceptional men. Exceptional, delicious, sexy, confident," she whispered, showering light kisses on his throat and shoulder and down on his chest.

His arms tightened around her, and he turned her face up to his, and she saw the desire that had rekindled in his eyes. He pulled her closer in his arms and kissed her, pushing her down on the bed and leaning over her.

She wound her arm around his neck and her other hand ran down his smooth, muscled back, down to his firm buttocks. She was still astounded she was in bed with him, being loved by him.

"Darlin', I think you've demolished me," he drawled in a sleepy voice.

She laughed softly. "I hope I have burned you to cinders."

Smiling at her, he rolled onto his back, pulling her against him with one arm around her waist while he toyed with her hair with his other hand.

"Erin, darlin', you're wonderful," he whispered.

She kissed his shoulder, and his arm tightened while his hand combed through her hair and then danced over her back to her buttocks, then down along her thigh.

"I guess you're not too demolished," she whispered when his arousal pressed against her.

"Yes, I am, but you're fanning fires back to life," he said in a husky voice, "but we'll wait."

He fell asleep in her arms and Erin's lids soon closed and she was asleep.

Some time later, she woke and stirred, momentarily disoriented as she started to stretch and felt a warm body against her. The arm around her waist tightened, pulling her close. Her eyes flew wide as memory crashed over her.

Three

She shifted away to look down at the man beside her. Boone Devlin. Her face flushed, and she felt hot all over to remember the night and how she had willingly fallen into his arms and into his bed.

Why had she been so easy? As quickly as she asked herself the question, she knew the answer. The man was sexy, seductive, irresistible.

She had never before been tempted like last night. Through high school, college and the years afterward—she was twenty-six years old and a virgin until Boone. What had been so magical and seductive about him? She knew the answers to that question. Each facet of the man bewitched her.

And she had had wine, something she was unaccustomed to, and at the time, something she didn't think she was feeling. But looking back now, she knew the glasses of wine had had an effect on her.

If she hadn't had a drop of wine, would she still have let

him seduce her? She wriggled away enough to turn on her side, prop her head up and look down at him.

She had lost her virginity to Boone after being so careful for so many years. Why did he seem so special, his lovemaking so right? Was she sorry? She knew she wasn't.

His thick lashes were feathered against his cheeks. He was definitely the most handsome man she had ever known. And from the first moment there had been a chemistry between them. She had not imagined the attraction. It had been mutual and no wine had been involved early in the evening.

His wavy brown hair was tangled, locks falling over his forehead, and she wanted to run her fingers through his hair. She wanted to kiss him, to wake him and make love again. At the same time, she was appalled that she had gone to bed with him the first night she had met him.

Then she remembered his remarks about marriage: never been married, not married, never will be. He had told her up front his feelings on commitment. She felt a little sick, yet at the same time, half of her wanted to lean down and kiss him awake and love him again.

When had she turned into this wanton sex-starved woman? But it wasn't sex-starved per se. It involved totally the man beside her. Was there such a thing as love at first sight? She didn't believe it and never had. That was the stuff of fairy tales, not real life and ordinary people.

Clamping her lips closed, she started to slip out of bed. His arm snaked out and wrapped around her, pulling her close against him, and he leaned over to kiss her.

She pushed against him. "Boone, wait—"

"Shh, darlin'," he whispered in return. "C'mere. I need you," he said softly, nuzzling her neck, and then he kissed her while she started to protest.

"Boone, let go," she said, and scrambled out of bed, looking frantically for something to cover her nakedness. She yanked up a pillow and discovered he was on his side, his head propped on his hand, enjoying watching her. With lithe ease, he slid out of bed and reached for her.

She backed away. "You stay away from me, you devilish charmer."

She could see the amusement dancing in his eyes, and she was struggling to control her own inclination to walk back into his arms. "Where are my clothes?" she snapped, telling herself that she should show some restraint. Her head was throbbing, and he was ignoring her, moving closer as she backed up.

He was naked, aroused, incredible. Male, virile, he was all hard muscles and she was having a difficult time with her protests.

"Come here, Erin," he coaxed in a seductively low voice. "Come here, darlin' and let's kiss again."

"You seduced me last night!"

"Might have, but as I recall, we both had a pretty great time."

Trying to back up and at the same time keep him at arm's length, she glanced over her shoulder to look for her discarded clothing.

"*I'm* a devilish charmer? You'll turn my head, darlin'. I didn't dream I had that effect on you."

"You know darn good and well you had that effect on me and you're laughing at me right now. I'm trying to do what I should and you're not making it easier." She glanced frantically over her shoulder and saw her clothes in a heap right beside the door. She looked back at him and he was even closer, reaching out to put his hand on her waist. She put one hand against his chest and held the pillow tightly against her with the other.

"I didn't have my wits about me last night!" she exclaimed, wondering how long she could keep them now. Her pulse was racing, and he was impossibly enticing.

"And I took advantage of you? Is that what you're accusing me of?"

"No! I know you didn't take advantage of me," she said, trying to back up and bumping a table, edging around it. "But I wasn't thinking as clearly as I should have been."

"And this means you're filled with regrets today. Do you regret last night, darlin'?"

His blue eyes nailed her and even while she could see amusement dancing in his eyes, she knew he was halfway earnest with his question. "You know I can't regret it, but I'm not doing it again!"

"Doing what again? Making hot, sexy love? Eating with me? Sleeping in my arms? Showering with me? What?"

"You think this whole thing is funny—"

"No, no!" he protested, suddenly looking solemn. "I'm as earnest about you and me as that sunshine outside. I know exactly what I want this morning, and there's nothing comical about it."

"You're pursuing me," she leveled at him.

"Damn straight there, sweetie. I am pursuing you and intend to continue to pursue you whatever you decide to do."

Her pulse jumped with his answer even though she didn't want it to.

She waved her hand at him. "Now, you stay right there and let me get my clothes and you just turn around. You don't need to watch and embarrass me."

"I would never dream of embarrassing you, not ever. But now to watch, darlin', I'll be drooling if I do that."

"You're going to stay there and nothing more!" she snapped, and reached down to scoop up her dress.

He moved closer, putting his fists against the door on either side of her and hemming her in. He stood only inches from her, and her heart was thudding loudly enough for him to hear. His hair was tangled over his forehead, he was totally naked and aroused, and she wanted to wrap her arms around him more than anything on earth, but common sense said not to do it.

She was clinging to her resistance the way she was clinging to the pillow in her arms, but she was doing better with the pillow. He was too close, his eyes too blue, his body too sexy.

"The most beautiful, feistiest redhead in the whole world is in my room and has spent the night in my arms," he drawled in a lazy, husky voice that took her breath. Every nerve in her body tingled and she ached for him, heat making her feel she was standing in the middle of an inferno.

"You just step away and don't start that seduction stuff," she ordered in a breathless voice that sounded as firm as soup.

"Seduction stuff? Surely I have more finesse than that," he replied in a low voice and brushed a kiss on her neck.

"You're not doing what I asked."

"That's because I don't think your whole heart is in that request to ask me to step away."

"I know you're laughing at me and I've been easy—"

"Darlin', there is nothing about you that is easy, I promise you that one." He was dusting kisses all along her throat and on her ear, his warm breath tickling her ear while one hand caressed her nape.

"Everything about me has been easy," she whispered, knowing she was losing the battle.

"Believe me, it hasn't. I want you to stay with me. C'mon, darlin', stay with me now." His hand slipped beneath the pillow to caress her breast, his thumb drawing circles on her nipple while he kissed her protests away.

Dimly she knew he pulled the pillow out of her arms and then he was holding her naked body pressed against his. He was warm, hard, ready.

She slipped one arm around his neck and capitulated totally, wanting him with all her being.

His kiss was devastating. She shouldn't fall right into his arms and his bed, but, oh, what kisses!

She kissed him, clinging to him, pressed against his warm, nude body and held tightly in his arms. How long they kissed, she didn't know, but finally she pushed slightly against his chest. "Boone, this is crazy. Last night I had wine and didn't—"

"Shh," he whispered, kissing her briefly and stopping her conversation. "The wine doesn't matter. It didn't have a thing to do with what's between us. I'll show you, darlin'." He tightened his arm and kissed her while his other hand caressed her breast. She moaned, the sound caught in her throat, muffled by their kisses.

He leaned away. "I want you, Erin. And I want you to stay with me this morning if you will," he said earnestly, and all amusement vanished from his expression, replaced by so much desire in his eyes that it took her breath.

Her heart thudded because she knew if she said no now and walked out, he would step back and let her go. She had to make a choice here. All her life she had known what she wanted and didn't want. She knew now what she *really* wanted.

She didn't want to walk away from this man who had turned her world topsy-turvy, the first man in her life to set her heart pounding. The best-looking man she had ever known, as well as the most exciting. He was silent, waiting, letting her make her choice.

She stood on tiptoe, tightened her arm around his neck and drew his head down to kiss him.

With their lips almost touching, she paused to whisper, "Someday I may regret this moment, but right now it seems perfect."

"Ah, darlin'," he said. "Do you hurt too much to make love again?"

"No." She pulled him closer.

And then they kissed. His hand slid down over her thigh, down between her legs, and she gasped and shifted her hips, giving him access to her.

"Boone," she whispered before words and reason vanished. She caressed and kissed him, tracing her hands over his muscled back, down over his firm buttocks. He groaned and pulled her close in his arms and she leaned down to take his shaft in her hand and kiss him, her tongue stroking him in hot, wet kisses.

He shook and she was amazed by the effect she had on him. He hauled her close against him and leaned down to kiss her long and passionately again, and rational or not, it seemed so right to be in his arms and loving him.

They kissed and caressed until he picked her up and carried her back to bed to make love to her. Using protection, he held her while he lowered himself to possess her.

"Boone!" she cried, wanting him, knowing she might have to reassess her feelings about people falling in love the first time they meet.

"This time is special for you," he whispered, moving slowly, withdrawing and then easing into her to fill her.

She cried out in a frenzy as she was driven to a need that set her quivering. "Boone, love me! Love me now!" she exclaimed. "I want you!"

Boone continued to go slowly, sweat beading his forehead and breaking out on his back and chest while he fought for control to try to pleasure her as much and as long as he could.

"Ah, Erin, darlin'!" he gasped, and felt his control slipping. "I can't wait longer, love," he whispered, and then he was beyond control. He dimly heard her cry above the roaring of his pulse when he crashed over a brink and had a shuddering release.

Erin gradually slowed, clinging to him. Her breathing and her heart rate returned to normal. She was damp with sweat and so was Boone. And she was swamped with the clear knowledge there was no way to blame this on wine.

He was showering her face and neck with light kisses. "You're wonderful, darlin'," he whispered.

She heard all his words of endearment, but she knew this was a man with a long history of women in his life. He was a handsome charmer, and she didn't have to ask to guess about other females' reactions to him. She was certain he said the same thing to others in similar circumstances. In spite of logic and knowledge, her resistance had been as forceful as mush.

He framed her face with his hands, and she gazed up into his blue eyes. "Stop worrying," he said. "What we have between us is awesome. We'll shower, go eat breakfast and drive to the ranch where you can show me around. All right?"

She suspected he was asking for a whole lot more than what he had just listed. She had a feeling she was going to make a commitment with her answer if it was affirmative.

"Erin, you're too full of life to have to think this one over."

"All right. You're a magician and you've cast a spell."

"No spells. Just a guy who thinks you're pretty super." He smiled at her, and she couldn't resist smiling in return.

They showered and Erin went to her room to get her things.

She changed into jeans and a green shirt, and when she joined him, he gazed at her appreciatively. "You look gorgeous! Yummy enough to peel you right out of those jeans and that shirt—"

"No you don't! I'm starving in spite of having had a steak late last night."

He grinned and picked up his wallet to put it into his hip pocket. "Let's go feed you, beautiful woman." Erin knew she would never again see the hotel without remembering Boone Devlin and last night and this morning.

In the hotel coffee shop he sat across from her as sunshine spilled through the window. "Tell me about the ranch," he said. "How long have you been manager?"

"For the past four years. My dad was ill my last year in college, and as soon as I graduated I came home and really began to take over then. He lived about six months after that."

Boone reached over to take her hand, folding hers in his large one. "Sorry about that. I know some of what it means. When my dad died, I had to go to work to help Mom with the other kids. I had to be daddy for them." He paused. Then, "Have you ever thought of leaving the ranch?"

"No! That's my home and has been home to several generations of my family. The Frates family has owned it back since settling there before the midnineteenth century. My family settled on the ranch at the same time, working for the Frates. That's my heritage and my tie to my family, and Mary and I are the last Fryes. My sister doesn't care a thing for it and couldn't wait to get away. But the Double T is important to me."

Boone hoped his features were impassive, because he could see trouble looming. How would Erin react to his plans to sell the ranch?

"The Double T Ranch is my life," she said firmly, looking beyond him, and he wondered if she had forgotten his presence. Her green eyes were wide, crystal clear, and now he knew how they darkened with passion. Just looking at her, he wanted to kiss her again. He couldn't remember any woman who had appealed to him the way Erin did. She had let him take her virginity. That awed him. They'd both had a lot of wine, but he suspected the wine didn't make that much difference. To think he was the only man she had ever been intimate with was stunning and made him surprisingly pleased and faintly possessive toward her.

"Where did the Double T name come from?"

"Tall Timbers was what it was originally called, and they used the two T's for a brand, so gradually, the ranch came to be called the Double T. That's how it's known today."

While she relayed some of the history of the ranch and made some remarks about her ancestors, he sipped hot, black coffee and listened.

Their omelettes came, and as they ate, she continued to tell him about famous horses from their ranch. He listened and half heard what she said, but most of his concentration was purely on her. She looked gorgeous this morning, dewy-eyed, her cheeks pink, looking as if she had slept soundly all night long.

"You might as well turn in your rental car and ride with me," Erin said.

"I'd like that," he said.

As soon as they finished eating, they checked out of the hotel.

At the airport, he returned his rental car to the agency and climbed into a black pickup with her. She drove through San Antonio's maze of streets that followed nineteenth-century wagon and cattle trails, while Boone watched her drive. What was the chemistry boiling between them that was too strong for either of them to resist?

"Do you train the horses?"

"No," she said, smiling. "We have wonderful trainers. I know some of what they do because I grew up following them around, but I deal mostly with the business part, meeting and dealing with buyers, occasionally going to horse sales—which is where I was for the past two days. You were wrong with your guess that I worked in the television industry."

"So I was. In a million tries it wouldn't have occurred to me that you managed a ranch."

She laughed. "I can imagine what you'd conjured up in your mind about the manager."

"Believe me, nothing even remotely as breathtaking and gorgeous as the real thing. Now, maybe as feisty—that comes closer to what I imagined."

"No one before you has ever described me as feisty."

"That's the way I see you."

"Well, you won your bet last night—I willingly told you my name. And you've collected, because I've told you far more than four new facts about me."

"Now I want to know a million—everything," he said, and she flashed him a quick dimpled smile.

As she drove, he looked at the passing landscape of lush, green hills that held wildflowers and oak. "This is pretty country."

"It's beautiful country, and lately we've had rainfall, so the hills are green."

"What are your plans for the future of the ranch?"

"That depends on you," she said, sliding him a saucy glance. "You're the new owner."

"If John Frates were still alive, what would your plans be?"

She shrugged. "To continue as we have in the past. We have excellent stock, superior bloodlines, a fully developed marketing program. It's a profitable operation, which you'll see."

"Any business connected to John Frates seemed to be a profitable operation," Boone remarked dryly. "Are you raising these horses to race or for ranching?"

"Most of our horses are sold to ranchers as working horses, but we've had about a fourth that have been bought with racing in mind. We're not specifically breeding for it, though."

He put his hand on her knee. "Careful," she cautioned. "I need to concentrate on my driving."

"I distract you that much?" he asked, arching an eyebrow.

She gave him another quick glance. "You know darn well you do."

"Is this less distracting?" he said, stretching his arm across the seat to caress her nape.

"No, and you know that, too! Do *you* want to drive?"

He smiled. "Not unless you're tired of driving."

"I thought maybe that's why you were trying to distract me."

"Hardly. I wasn't trying to distract you. I just want my hands on you—even if it is casual."

"Nothing is casual with you," she said softly, and his pulse jumped another notch.

"Let's go dancing tomorrow night," he said. "It's Friday."

She laughed. "You don't waste any time! The minute we go dancing, we'll be the talk of the county."

"Do you care?"

She thought that over while she drove. "I guess I don't. All right, Boone, we'll go dancing tomorrow night."

"Great! I'm not sure I want to wait until Friday."

"That's just tomorrow. You can wait. So, tell me, why is it that you'll never marry?"

He had a feeling that any future relationship he wanted with her might be hanging in the balance here, but he had always been honest with the women he dated and he didn't want to change that now.

"Earlier I told you about my dad's death and how I became daddy and head of the household. I've raised eight kids because my mom worked two jobs to support us. I've had diapers and runny noses and juggling bills and giving up what I wanted to do until the next one got old enough to step in and help. Actually, it wasn't the next one because that's a brother who's as flighty as they come. Anyway, I want my freedom. I've been there and done the family scene. I'm not into commitment, marriage or long-term relationships."

"That's plainspoken. I wasn't contemplating walking down the aisle with you. I was just curious because you sounded emphatic."

When she became silent, he wondered if she regretted last night. If anyone looked the type for marriage it was Erin.

"Tell me about your years in Special Forces," she said, glancing at him. "That sounds like a wild life."

"I was trained for it and it was certainly challenging. I was a chopper pilot. Flying is one of the great loves of my life, so being able to serve my country and help others while being a pilot was great."

"You *did* help others. You saved John."

Boone talked about his military background a little and then asked her questions about the ranch, realizing her life was wrapped up in the Double T.

She told him about neighbors and people in the county and the people who worked on the ranch. Finally they reached land that had an antiquated-looking wooden fence stretching in the distance.

"Here's where boundaries for the ranch start," she informed him, and he gazed out over more hills, then his view was blocked by thick stands of oak. He was amazed by the size of the place even though he had read about the amount of acreage, but to see it made it real.

"Do you have any boots, Boone?"

"Yes, I do. I come from a Kansas farm. This isn't totally new to me."

"We do have snakes. You're in the flying business, so the ranch must hold little interest for you. John Frates was here maybe twice a year. What do you plan to do?"

Her question hung in the air while Boone contemplated his answer. This was the moment to break it to her that he considered selling the ranch.

Four

Glancing into his blue eyes, she wondered what he had planned to do with the ranch, and when the silence grew, she realized it was something he didn't want to tell her.

"I'm thinking about talking you into selling," he admitted in a solemn tone.

A chill ran down her spine, yet she plastered a smile on her face. "And you were confident you could convince me to agree, right? Since according to the will, I have to agree before you can sell the place."

"I'm aware of that," he replied. "I'm going to have to rethink some things. You're not what I was expecting."

"Why would you want to sell the ranch? It's highly profitable."

"I'm interested in my air charter business, not a ranch. I'm interested in flying, as I said."

"But you can have both easily," Erin protested. "You're not essential to the ranch. John Frates was seldom here. You're not necessary in any way to running the place," she said quietly. "That's *my* job. Why would you want to give up something that can earn you big money year after year?"

"Because the Double T is worth a lot if I sell it, and I can take the money from the ranch and pour it into my business."

"You're not exactly without funds," she pointed out. "I know the terms of John's will."

"At the moment I'm postponing things because right now—" his voice lowered seductively as he drew his finger slowly from her wrist to her shoulder "—I'm in no hurry to leave Texas."

Trying to ignore the zinging current from his light touch, she slanted him a quick look. The obvious desire in his expression confirmed what he'd said.

"When did you start your air charter business?"

"When I got out of the military a couple of years ago. It's new, but it's growing and keeps me busy and I've hired four more pilots and bought another plane. I've got orders for two more planes."

"Who runs the business while you're here?"

"I've got a buddy, Mason Sloane, who works for me, and he's in charge in my absence. I can count on him. Actually, I can count on any employee who works for me. My guys are a reliable bunch."

"So are the ranch hands. Some of them are like I am— fourth or fifth generation to work on the ranch."

"You're young and beautiful—"

She wrinkled her nose at him in protest.

"Why do you want to bury yourself out on a remote ranch? Don't you want to date, get married, see the world, do things?" Boone asked.

"I don't want to leave it. I told you, the ranch is my life. It's exciting and a challenge and my tie to my family and the past."

"I'm surprised he didn't will you the ranch."

"John told me many times that he expected me to marry and move away. My sister was gone as soon as possible."

"He didn't protect your interests very well."

"Yes, he did. You have to have my permission to sell the Double T," she reminded him. "That protects my interest."

"I'm also surprised you didn't make some effort to buy it yourself."

She shook her head and her thick, red hair swirled across her shoulders and he couldn't resist sliding his arm over to wind his fingers in her silky locks. With an effort he tried to pay attention to what she was saying and keep his mind off memories of the night.

"I like being solvent," she explained. "I have a trust and I get a generous salary, plus a commission from the ranch. The money I make is more than adequate, in addition to a comfortable inheritance. No, I have no inclination to purchase the ranch."

Boone half listened as she gave him histories of the most spectacular horses raised on the ranch. He heard names—Gypsy Runner, White Wind, but his thoughts were on Erin.

Erin totally captivated him. He wanted her in his bed tonight and he suspected there was little he could do if she did not want to be there. He couldn't ever recall spending a night with a woman that held the excitement and intensity of last night. And he couldn't ever recall a woman walking away after one night with him. He had always been the one to walk away.

From the first few moments in the parking lot, Erin had been unpredictable, and he suspected that wasn't going to change any time in the near future. She slowed, and he stopped watching her to shift his attention to the open gates to the ranch.

Supporting the gates, two stacked stone columns rose high into the air with a metal arch connecting them. A wooden sign bearing the Double T brand hung from the arch. As they drove over the cattle guard, Boone shifted uncomfortably. He had an uneasy premonition that his life was about to change again. And maybe in a manner he couldn't control. He shrugged away the feeling, something he hadn't experienced for years. In his adult life he had been in control of most situations and when he hadn't been in control, he had been working hard to get control of whatever he was involved in.

They sped along a hard-packed dirt road until she slowed to top a rise. At the foot of it, one end of a broken bridge lay smashed in a rushing creek. The other end of the bridge was still secure.

"There's the reason they told me to avoid trying to get home last night and just stay in a hotel in town."

"Good reason, and I'm grateful to a rainstorm and a fallen bridge."

Erin left the road and drove down the embankment, the car sliding in the mud. At the bottom, she forded the creek. Outside, tumbling muddy water came halfway up the tires. Boone watched her handle the pickup with ease that he knew was old stuff to her. She impressed him besides the wild attraction that burned between them.

"This creek was up over the bridge last night?" he asked.

"Hard to imagine, isn't it? And now it's down again," she said, driving through the creek and returning to the road on the other side.

In minutes, houses and other buildings of the ranch came into view. "There," she said, "is your new home. Seventeen thousand square feet of luxury, ten bedrooms and nine and a half baths. Like what you see?"

"I like what I see beyond my wildest imagination," he said

in a husky voice, and she shot a glance at him to find him staring at her.

"Look at your house, for heaven's sake!" she exclaimed while her cheeks became pink.

"This view is infinitely more fascinating, but I'll look." Turning, he saw the palatial grounds only partially visible through the trees surrounding the tended grounds that were divided by a tall, black wrought-iron fence from the wild pastureland on three sides and the driveway on the other.

"Holy Toledo!" he exclaimed, once again shocked by John Frates's wealth. The sprawling three-story house was certainly a mansion. "Was I ever off in my visions of this ranch and its manager!"

"I can well imagine," Erin remarked dryly.

Across from the house were the other structures. "There are three stables with their runs, our corral, a feed-storage building, an office, my house and our foreman's house. Two of the accountants live on the ranch, other employees have their own houses here. There's a bunkhouse, a shop, a track."

As she continued listing ranch structures, his gaze ran over three picturesque, rustic-looking stables constructed of aging, gray weathered boards.

In addition to the ranch house, he saw other sizable houses with attractive, landscaped and fenced yards stretching out of sight farther down one of the roads beyond the house. Roads splintered off in various directions from the main road.

"This looks like its own small town. Or not-so-small town," Boone remarked, stunned by the size of the place.

"We sort of are our own town," she replied. "The first house is my home. The one across the road is a guest house. The large Frates home is now yours."

"I can't imagine," he said quietly, eyeing the magnificent

structure that had wings in a U-shaped direction. "It still isn't real to me, and I can't see myself living in that mansion."

"It's yours to do with as you please. By the way, my house is a little island that was deeded to my grandfather years ago. Even though it is surrounded by the Double T, that little bit of land is mine."

"I remember. With the size of this place, your few acres hardly matter."

She passed his ten-car garage that held an assortment of vehicles. His gaze ran over an all-terrain vehicle, a shiny, black sports car, another pickup and a Jeep. She slowed and stopped in front of her own three-car garage. When they climbed out of the car, he took her bag out of the pickup and carried his own. As she walked around the car, he blocked her path.

"Give me your things. I'll carry them," he said, taking another bag from her hand and remaining immobile, still blocking her way. "Erin, come stay with me tonight," he said solemnly.

She blinked, uncertainty and concern filling her green eyes. Sunlight caught glints of gold in her red hair. The vision of her gazing back at him in silence would be etched in his memory for a long time to come, he was sure. He was surprised how important her answer was to him.

"I'll have to think that one over," she replied. "You want me tonight, tomorrow you may be gone."

His heart sank. It was the answer he dreaded and had half expected. "Darlin', I want you in my arms tonight."

Again, she stared at him so long that it made him nervous and feeling as if he were about sixteen and asking a girl to the prom, only this was more important than any prom.

"Slow down, Boone. This is new to me, and I need to think things through. I know you're not into commitment of any kind. While I'm not asking for commitment, I'm also not into casual, so I have to give your request some thought before I answer."

"Erin, there is nothing casual about my request."

To his surprise, she laughed. "Get serious! Loving women is all casual to you and a game. C'mon. I'll show you around your new acquisition. You're lord of the manor now."

She sashayed past him quickly, and he stared after her in consternation. He hurried to catch up. "Dammit, Erin, I'm serious. It—"

"Don't even try to deny what I said," she warned him. "If you must have an answer right now, the answer is—"

He put his fingers on her lips. "Don't say no. I can wait," he said with a sigh. "Show me around."

He saw the twinkle in her eyes and wanted to gnash his teeth or grab her and kiss her, except he knew that would not help his cause.

He didn't think she took him seriously one iota and he was not accustomed to such a reaction from any woman, much less one he had just made love to the night before. A virgin. She had been passionate beyond his wildest dreams. Why wasn't she all starry-eyed today?

He laughed silently at himself. You pompous jackass, he thought, yet he couldn't keep from being disgruntled, off balance, and piqued by her reactions. And attracted more than ever. She turned and headed toward her house, and he watched the sexy sway of her hips. Taking a deep breath, he hurried to catch up with her.

He reached around her to unlatch and swing open a white wooden gate. The yard was beautifully landscaped and he was certain watered by a sprinkler system. Beds of trimmed flowers bloomed profusely. He looked at red and pink roses, brilliant fuchsia and purple crepe myrtle. Pots of red hibiscus

decorated the wraparound porch that held white wicker furniture, hanging pots of green ivy and ferns. She went up the
steps and unlocked the front door and he followed her inside.

The house looked like her. The wide hallway was cozy, appealing, surprising with an eclectic collection of art that
ranged from a Klee contemporary to a Gilbert Stuart oil to
Remington bronzes, with some unknown artists included.

He paused in front of the Stuart oil, staring at it.

"It's an original," she said from behind him as she set her
purse on a credenza. "Art is my weakness. I fly to London
once a year for an art auction. My grandfather got me
started—he collected, and I've added to it."

Setting down her bags, Boone stared at her and realized
he had been a million miles off in the image he had conjured
up of the manager of the horse ranch. An annual trek to a London art auction? He was all the more intrigued with her, this
dazzling woman who made his pulse pound.

"Are you going to give me a tour?" he asked.

"Of my house? That can come later. I just stopped off here
to put my things down. Let's go and take the grand tour of
your new house."

He wanted to drop his flight bag and take her into his
arms, but he suspected she would nix that action, so he merely
walked to the door with her. He held it open and stepped out
onto the porch behind her, hearing the lock click when he
closed the door.

They crossed the wide driveway and went through a black
wrought-iron gate and up a walk to a house with six huge
Ionic columns across the front and a ten-foot, hand-carved
double front door with a high fan transom above it.

She unlocked the door, stepped inside and turned off the
alarm. He followed her inside, looking from the marble floor
in the hallway to a dazzling chandelier that hung from the

eighteen-foot ceiling. The elegant decor of original oils, statues, exotic plants and carved mahogany furniture was breathtaking. Boone couldn't imagine being owner until he stepped into a spacious family room that was so warm and welcoming he instantly took a liking to the house.

"This is great," he said, relieved to see comfortable brown leather furniture, a polished plank floor with oriental area rugs, a big-screen television, more mahogany furniture and shelves filled with books.

"I thought you'd like it," she answered, standing at the floor-to-ceiling glass doors that opened onto a patio and a sparkling sixty-foot, blue-tiled pool flanked on one side by masses of blooming rose of Sharon bushes.

Boone stepped up behind her, running his hands over her shoulders and turning her to face him.

"What I like is you," he said quietly. "At least let's have dinner together. There has to be something in this palace that I can throw together."

"You'll have maid service. You won't have to throw anything together," she said. "The staff isn't here this morning because I didn't know when you would get in. I'll contact them, and you can meet them this afternoon," she said, pulling out her cell phone and punching numbers. He listened to her give orders efficiently as he roamed around the room and wandered outside by the enormous pool that had a fountain in the center and a waterfall at one end. He turned to watch Erin step outside and approach him.

"We're eating here alone tonight?"

Smiling, she nodded. "That's what you said you wanted."

He rested his hands on her shoulders and combed his fingers in her hair.

He wanted to lean down and kiss her, but as he looked intently at her, she wriggled away and was gone.

"Let's go look upstairs and you can select your bedroom," she said, slanting him a sultry look over her shoulder that had him tied in knots. He was hot and bothered and wanting her to a degree that surprised him. There was always a pretty woman. Why get tied in knots over this one?

Trailing after her, he caught up as she crossed the family room and went down the hall to a sweeping staircase. "There is an elevator in the back part of the house if you ever get tired of the stairs, but I'd doubt if you will want to use it."

"No, I won't," he replied.

She showed him two enormous bedrooms before stepping into one that filled an upper floor of the south side of one wing of the house. Along with a balcony, the room held a magnificent, carved bed that looked like something out of another century. The massive stone fireplace added to the feeling of antiquity. A carved mahogany desk stood near one wall. He looked at the enormous television screen, shelves of books, a sitting area with a sofa and chairs and tables.

"The view here is the best in the house," she said, standing beside the floor-to-ceiling glass that made up one wall of the bedroom. Beyond her, Boone could see rolling, tree-covered acres of green ranch land.

Boone crossed the room to her and picked her up in his arms and carried her to the bed.

"Let's just sit on the edge of the bed and try out the mattress. Before you start protesting, I'm only holding you."

She regarded him with the same disinterested look as if she were humoring a willful child.

"So what do you think?" she asked cheerfully.

"I think I want to kiss you," he said, holding her close in his arms.

"No. What do you think about the mattress?" she asked while he nuzzled her neck.

"I think it's grand. Soft, warm, intoxicating…"

She laughed and slipped off his lap. "All right. I'll show you another bedroom."

"Which bedroom in this castle do you like the best?" he asked, standing and moving close to her again.

She looked around. "This one because it has the best view, lots of books, the fireplace, the beautiful landscape, the desk that is one of my favorite pieces in the house."

"This is my bedroom then."

"Fine. Come on, and we'll finish the tour."

As he walked out of the bedroom beside her, he said, "I'm astounded by the grandeur of this house. I've seen Mike's house and Jonah's. They inherited big, fine homes, but neither one of them are like the one I got."

"No. This one is about five years newer than either one of their houses and Great-Grandfather Frates poured the money into this one. It was the showplace of the Frates fortune. The horses were the love of Great-Grandfather Eben Frates, a love not shared by his son or grandson. He wanted this to be a showplace for people who came to buy the horses, and there have been some famous people here. It wasn't quarter horses back then, that specialty developed much later. It was just fine horses."

"Why wasn't it quarter horses?" Boone asked.

"Quarter horses are purely American and registration and all that began at a later time. There were thoroughbred horses here and fine breeding stock. He wanted this to be on par with castles of European royalty."

"European royalty came here to buy horses?"

"A few. You'll see the pictures of famous customers in the library and the office."

When they stepped into the library that was filled with shelves of books on two walls, Erin led Boone to a wall filled with pictures.

"These people bought horses here?" he said, looking at a picture he recognized of a man who had been president of the United States when Boone was a child. Boone spotted half a dozen movie actors and listened as Erin pointed out royalty and other celebrities.

"This is why Great-Grandfather Eben Frates, the original Frates, wanted a fancy, impressive house on this ranch. When you're more familiar with the ranch, you'll recognize the background of a lot of these pictures."

He caressed her nape. "It's impressive, and I guess you have some of the finest horses in the world, but it's difficult to get my attention on anything except the ranch manager."

"You'll manage," she answered briskly as if she was oblivious to his light caresses. "There are more pictures in the office. It's right down the hall."

He draped his arm across her shoulders and pulled her close beside him and wanted to kiss her more than he wanted to look at the house, but he suspected if he didn't pay attention to her guided tour, she would go home and leave him on his own.

He entered another large, rustic room that had two bearskins mounted on the walls, one behind an imposing, carved mahogany desk. Pictures of more celebrities and pictures of horses covered two walls.

It took over an hour to tour the house, to look at the formal dining room and living areas, including an exercise room, an indoor pool, a billiard room, a ten-seat home theater.

It was almost eleven when they left to tour the ranch.

As soon as they stepped into the stables, he paused and placed his hands on his hips as he took a long look around at the aging structure and the empty stalls.

"The stalls open into a large run so the horses can come and go, and we turn them out to pasture most of the time in good weather."

"You said John Frates wasn't here often. Now I believe it. Not that you aren't doing a great job, but these stables are old."

"That's their charm. They're the original stables," she said proudly. "These are over one hundred and thirty years old— one hundred and thirty-nine, to be exact—and built by both a Frates and a Frye as well as others who helped. Our foreman is my uncle, Perry Frye. The Fryes are linked to this ranch from the beginning."

Nodding, he followed her through the cool, dark stable and he could tell that she loved the building and was proud of it, but he thought it was an antiquated firetrap and something that needed to be replaced. He made a mental note to check into it.

As he looked at a well-stocked tack room, he knew he could get a marvelous price for the ranch. He gazed at Erin speculatively, wondering whether he could get her back into his bed or not. Wondering if he sold the ranch if he'd ever coax her into bed again.

The dawning realization that he could not entice her to stay with him still surprised him. To have a woman turn a cool shoulder to him the day after a night of passion was as difficult to accept as his continuing consuming desire for her. Past women would excite him for a night or two, but rarely longer.

"Are your eyes beginning to glaze over?" she asked, amused. "You don't have to involve yourself with all the details of horse breeding, training and marketing."

"I lived on a farm until I was twelve," Boone told her. "And I've ridden in rodeos in college in saddle bronc events. That's the extent of my experience with horses." If he sold the ranch, he wouldn't have to deal with the horses.

"As I told you, you don't have to involve yourself at all.

John and his family came here to relax and ride and enjoy the peace and quiet. You can leave the horses up to the ranch experts."

"Let me show you the horses," she said, and they left the stable to get into a black pickup. In a short time she stopped by a fenced pasture and he got out with her to climb onto the fence and look at the horses that ambled over, their satiny coats shiny in the bright sunlight. She had tidbits for them and showed him her horse, Mercury.

"About three mornings a week I ride at dawn. Want to join me some morning?" she asked.

"If we can get up together," he replied, arching his eyebrows and holding his breath for her answer.

She wrinkled her nose at him. "That's not part of the bargain," she said, her full lips curving in a smile and her dimple showing. "If you don't ride with me, you'll wish you had. It's beautiful and quiet and just marvelous."

"I want to. I just want to get up together to go for the ride."

"Well, you'll have to wait on that one," she said blithely, and hopped down off the fence. "C'mon. I'll show you some of our prize studs."

For another hour they looked at horses and then Erin drove to the highway and stopped at a small grocery store to purchase items for a picnic lunch. They climbed back into her pickup and drove to the ranch, where she left the ranch road, bouncing over open fields until they stopped beneath the shade of a spreading live oak.

She opened a blanket and in minutes they were seated in the shade eating sandwiches of cold cuts and drinking chilled bottles of pop. While she talked about growing up on the ranch and gave him more history of the place, dappled sunlight shone between leaves and caught golden highlights in her thick, red hair. She was warm and had unbuttoned her shirt and his eyes kept straying to the open vee of her green shirt.

He finally tangled his fingers in her hair and then in minutes was stroking her nape. As his fingers moved lightly over her smooth skin, his imagination ran wild and he remembered the night before. He was aroused, aching and wanting her badly.

To his consternation, she suddenly stood up, brushed herself off and gathered up their things. "Let's finish our tour," she said.

He stood to pick up the blanket and the rest of their things and turned to watch her walk to the pickup. She could put him off now, but she wasn't going to tonight. Not like this. He watched the slight sway of her hips, mentally stripping away her snug jeans.

"Damnation," he said under his breath, striding after her. He shouldn't be so tied in knots after a night of intense satisfaction, but he was.

Next, they drove across the ranch to a pasture where men were working on a stock tank. One separated from the others and approached them and she introduced Boone to her uncle, Perry Frye, the ranch foreman.

"Howdy. Is it Colonel Devlin or Mr. Devlin?" The short, sandy-haired older cowboy gave Boone a solid handshake.

"It's Boone. This is an impressive operation. More so than I imagined."

"Yes, sir. It's a fine ranch," Perry said. As they talked, Erin left them, moving away to talk to a group of men who were setting up a new stock tank.

"You plan to move to the ranch?" Perry asked, his blue eyes studying Boone intently.

"I'm thinking about it. I have an air charter business that I plan to continue, but I'm interested in finding out more about the ranch."

"Know much about quarter horses?"

"Next to nothing," Boone admitted, and Perry nodded. "I hope to learn," Boone said.

Perry spread his feet apart and folded his hands across his middle. "Erin was her daddy's darlin', and my niece is a special woman. He wouldn't have wanted to see her hurt."

Boone realized the drift of the conversation and that he was being quietly warned to avoid hurting Erin. He looked the older man in the eye. "She's already demonstrated a high degree of ability to take care of herself, and I have no intention of hurting her."

"Didn't think you would. Just remarking on it. She can take care of herself in some ways. Glad to have you here, Mr. Devlin."

"Call me Boone," he repeated.

"Anything I can do for you, let me know."

"I guess you can teach me about quarter horses."

Perry raked his fingers through his thick hair and jammed his hat back on his head. "If you want to go to work with me tomorrow, you'll learn a little about these horses. Meet me at the big kitchen at five tomorrow morning."

"Yes, sir. I'll do that," Boone answered, wanting to groan. He didn't want to meet Perry Frye at five in the morning and he didn't want to start learning about quarter horses before the sun came up on his second day on the ranch, but he also wanted to impress Erin and he suspected he had to earn the foreman's respect. He shook hands and turned to get Erin.

He met other cowboys who worked on the ranch and tried to memorize their names, knowing he would see them again in less than twenty-four hours. Back in the pickup with Erin, he told her about his 5:00 a.m. appointment and got a burst of laughter.

"You don't have to go work with Uncle Perry at five in the morning! He's just trying to scare you away probably."

"Why would he want to scare me away?" Boone asked, but knew the reason was sitting beside him.

"He's protective of me. He's like a second father. He probably sees you as a threat to my well-being."

"Well, damnation, why? You won't give me the time of day!"

She laughed. "I've given you a lot more than the 'time of day'!"

"It's becoming a long-ago memory."

"I told you that you'd forget all about me."

"You're taunting me, darlin'," he said in a low voice. "I haven't forgotten one tiny thing about last night. I remember how your lips feel when I kiss you," he said in a husky tone. "I remember how you moved your hips when—"

"Never mind!" she exclaimed, her cheeks turning pink.

"I don't want you to think I've forgotten anything. I recall in finest detail how soft you—"

"Boone! Stop that! I believe that you remember and I don't care to hear a recital!"

"Why not?" he drawled, his talk just making him want her more than ever. He didn't want to drop the subject because in a minute they would be back at the house and he had hopes of getting her to himself again and into his arms. Especially if he kept her mind on last night.

"You'll embarrass me."

"Embarrass you—or make you want to do all that again? Are you scared to hear about last night? I thought it was mighty great and I can't wait to make love to you. And when I do, I want to kiss you all over, darlin'. Slow, wet kisses," he said softly, drawing out his words and running his fingers along her arm and up to her nape to lightly caress her.

"Kisses that go—"

"Boone, stop now," she whispered. Her knuckles were

white as she gripped the steering wheel. "Stop or I'll have a wreck."

"There's nowhere out here to have a wreck, and no one else to get tangled up with. You're perfectly safe."

"The last thing I am is safe," she said through clenched teeth. "You stop trying to seduce me while I'm driving or I won't eat with you tonight or go out with you or anything else."

"One would think that you don't like me," he said matter-of-factly.

"I like you too darn well, and you just stop talking, and behave and keep your hands to yourself."

"Won't that dull things down a lot? Seems to me this is much more exhilarating." Once more, he drew his fingers lightly across her nape. "There. Doesn't that make you tingle? Would you rather have me ignore you and keep my hands to myself?"

"At the moment, yes," she replied, staring straight ahead.

He laughed softly. "All right. I'll wait until you're not driving.

When she flashed him a scalding look, his pulse jumped. She looked hot and flushed and desire had darkened her eyes. Her words had slowed and her breathing had become ragged, so he knew she was more aware of him than she indicated as she still blithely talked about ranch history and her family.

"Uncle Perry is widowed. Aunt Corrine had a fatal heart attack last year. He has two boys, Bret and Nick, who are in college."

"Any other relatives who work here?" Boone asked, and she shook her head.

When they got back to the house, he met three of the groundskeepers. Next, he met Nan and Gordy Barnes who cleaned, but it was the cook, Hettie Price, a gray-haired woman who gave him a steely-eyed look, and he suspected she was one more old family retainer who was protective of Erin.

Erin led him to the family room and turned to face him. "Now you've met most of the regular staff and some of the cowboys and our foreman. There are a lot more cowboys who work here and we have trainers plus two more who help with the grounds and one handyman who does a lot of house repairs. Hettie cooks for me two days a week."

He glanced at his watch. "It's after three. Let's go for a swim and then I'll put steaks on the grill tonight and we'll send this army of people home and have the place to ourselves."

"Thanks," Erin said, smiling at him as she began to move toward the door. "I need some time to catch up on things while I was away. If you want to eat dinner here tonight, I'll come back about half past six."

"I'll walk you home."

She laughed. "No need for that! I can't get lost. See you at half past six." She left the room, and he trailed after her, standing in the hall and watching her stride away.

He wondered if she was going to walk right out of his life after the greatest night he'd ever had.

He dismissed the help, telling them that he wouldn't need them for the evening or the next day. He didn't want cooks and cleaning people bustling around the house if he could get Erin to stay or join him in his room—an event that was beginning to seem highly unlikely.

He strode through the mansion, unable to feel like the owner. In another twenty minutes he was in the pool and swam as if he were getting ready for competition. He wanted to let off steam and get Erin out of his thoughts and try to cool down, hoping to exhaust himself.

By a quarter after six, his pulse raced as he went out a side door, crossed the lawn and headed toward her house, determined that she would not be so evasive and aloof this evening. Seduction of the most luscious and interesting woman he had ever known was his goal for tonight.

Five

Erin brushed her hair, studying her image while butterflies tickled her insides. She tried to bank her eagerness. Dismayed how easily she had fallen into Boone's arms and into his bed last night, she could not keep from being giddy and nervous about being with him again.

She tried to remind herself that Boone probably caused that hot chemistry with every woman he focused his attention on. But Erin knew that she couldn't move into his bed and his life after one wild night of passion. She had to slow down and gather her wits and see what she really wanted before it turned out to be a broken heart when Boone moved on.

But, oh, how difficult it had been to keep him at arm's length all day when all she had wanted was to walk right back into his arms and let him make wild, passionate love to her! The thought of the night before heated her up as well as any fire.

His body was masculine perfection and he was a consummate, considerate lover.

"How would you know?" she asked her image, wrinkling her nose. After all, he was her only lover. Yet she knew she was right. All the more reason to be cautious and careful.

She studied her reflection intently, trying to see herself through Boone's eyes. She wore a turquoise cotton sundress with spaghetti straps, a full skirt and a narrow leather belt. She slipped her bare feet into sandals. A dab of perfume behind her ears and on her throat and wrist gave her a light, flowery scent.

She caught her hair up on either side of her head with clips. She had already changed outfits three times and she was not going to change again. Did she look too plain? Too country? He was cosmopolitan and worldly. The house had awed him somewhat, but only briefly, and then he seemed to accept it as easily as if it had been a six-room bungalow.

His knowledge of quarter horses was slim, but he really didn't need to know anything. John Frates hadn't known a lot about them, either.

The worry nagged her that Boone might sell the ranch. He obviously preferred his charter service. Once, right after John Frates's death, she and her uncle had discussed going in together to try to buy the place. Neither wanted the debt. She rubbed her forehead, worrying about the future of the Double T and her own future as its manager.

How long would Boone stay? If she accepted his invitation, he might stay for a time. She might persuade him he should keep the Double T. If she didn't, she guessed he would be gone within a week. There was nothing here for him, and he had a business already.

Hettie looked as if she wanted to chase him off the place instantly. Erin smiled as she put diamond studs in her ears. The cook was protective and probably didn't approve of Boone since she'd found out he hadn't grown up in Lago or

Piedras counties, or even in Texas for that matter, and that seemed to be the ultimate requirement for Hettie.

Erin checked her watch and glanced out the window to see Boone walking across the lawn. She moved closer to the window to watch his long-legged stride that covered the ground swiftly.

Excitement escalated in her and all her caution melted like ice cream beneath hot fudge. He wore navy slacks and a navy knit shirt and he was handsome enough to scramble her wits. How could she keep this man at arm's length?

She wanted to rush downstairs and into his arms. Instead, she took a deep breath and thought about the broken hearts he probably had in his past, the women he had been dating only a week ago—or a couple of nights ago. The thoughts cooled her slightly, but not enough to be real proof against his charms.

With another deep breath she left her room, going through the house and then pausing, having no intention of rushing to meet him no matter how badly she wanted to.

She walked sedately to the front door, opening it and catching her breath because at close range he was even more devastating.

"Hi," he said, his warm gaze taking her in. "I thought I'd walk you to my house. You look gorgeous."

"Thank you," she replied, closing the door behind her. He took her hand, which surprised her. "You're going to send shock waves across the ranch," she said.

"How so?" he asked, looking down at her.

"Holding my hand. We're out in plain sight and maybe no one will see us, but more than likely someone will and then rumors will fly over the Double T like wildfire."

"You haven't ever walked around holding hands with a guy before?"

"Not since I brought a friend home one year when I was in college and I don't think we held hands, but I did bring him home to meet my dad."

"How serious were you?"

"Not too serious. We dated for about six months that year and then the relationship fizzled. There never has been anyone else."

"I find that most amazing except I still think it's because you're buried out here with the horses."

"I'm not buried. It's my life."

"So do you mind rumors flying?"

She shook her head and smiled at him, her eyes twinkling. "I don't mind. But you better watch out. Between Hettie and Uncle Perry, you should be careful. They'll give you a hard time and may try to run you off."

"So it's not me personally. It's any guy who steps in?"

"Well, sort of. If you were a Texan and from this county and a rancher or someone who had grown up in these parts and would always live and work here, then you would have passed some major hurdles. There would always be obstacles—questions about the usual character qualities."

"Hettie isn't your mother and Uncle Perry isn't your father."

"They think they're substitutes and doing what they should do since I no longer have a mother or father to protect me."

"Whoo," he said, shaking his head. "I can't recall any female who had to be protected from me—maybe one or two protected by me, but not from me. You'd think I'd sprouted fangs. Don't they know there's a world outside of Texas?"

"Is there really?"

He grinned and pulled her close against him. "All right then. Let's give them something to worry about and they can just start protecting you from my fearsome presence," he said, leaning down to kiss her.

He had caught her off guard and her first inclination was to step back, but it transformed into a whole different impulse. His tongue went deep and her insides clenched while her temperature soared and all the banked feelings she had tried to squelch through the day burst into scalding needs.

She wasn't aware of wrapping her arms around his neck. She wasn't aware of the ranch or that they were standing in front of his gate or that she was tossing aside her defenses and letting down all barriers. The caution she had fought to preserve throughout the day was evaporating, disappearing beneath hot kisses that made her melt, her knees turn to jelly.

Combing her fingers in his hair, she held him close. She trembled with desire as she kissed him, putting all her longing into her kiss, wanting to drive herself into his memory where she wouldn't be just another dazzled female in a long line of conquests.

How long did they stand and kiss? She didn't know because time ceased. Finally, though, beyond the driving need that was consuming her, reason whispered. Reluctantly, she struggled to regain control of her actions. She pushed against his chest and then shoved more forcefully, twisting away to look up at him.

Their breathing was ragged and for a few seconds they could only stare at each other. Pinpoints of fire in his blue eyes relayed his desire while his fingers toyed with her hair. With a racing pulse, she took his hand to lead him toward the house.

"Come on. We've probably sent someone into shock and talk will be all over the county by this time tomorrow. We'll hope Uncle Perry doesn't come after you with a shotgun."

"That went out with buggies and muzzle-loading rifles," Boone replied.

"Not around here."

He walked beside her and they went through the gate and across the lawn in silence. She glanced at him, wondering about his uncustomary quietness.

"You're at a loss for words. I'm surprised."

"We'll get inside and talk," he said in a tight voice, and she knew she was going to have to make a decision because he sounded solemn.

As soon as he closed the imposing front door behind him, he caught her hand to pull her around to face him. He placed his hands on her shoulders. "I want you, Erin. Move in with me. I want you here tonight, tomorrow night, every night in my arms."

With a pounding heart she gazed into his eyes and knew that while he sounded as if he wanted a long-term commitment, he could not possibly mean it. He had firmly declared he was not into commitment and he never would marry. As handsome as he was, she guessed he went from woman to woman easily.

Did she want to be seduced into his bed on his terms? Did she want to move into his bed at all? Her racing heart was her answer. She wanted to say yes and walk back into his arms and continue kissing him, but she knew that was the path to heartbreak. At least think it over, she told herself.

She placed her hands on his cheeks. "You're rushing me, and this is a big step. Give me a little time, Boone, long enough that I'm sure about what I'm doing."

He groaned and pulled her to him to kiss her hungrily, leaning over her and wrapping one arm tightly around her waist and tangling the other hand in her hair. Her heart thudded while she lost track of her argument. His fingers played down over her throat, pushing away a spaghetti strap and reaching down to cup her breast. He pushed away her lacy bra and his thumb circled her nipple.

Erin moaned, sensations rocking her and making her want him more than ever. Kissing her throat, he tugged down the zipper of her dress and pushed the top away so he could kiss her breast. His tongue circled her nipple and she gasped, her fingers tensing as one hand tugged his shirt out of his slacks. Her hand slipped beneath his shirt and she moved her fingers across his muscled chest. His chest was hard, warm, marvelous, and she wanted to keep touching and kissing him even though she knew it was contrary to what she had just told him.

She could feel his arousal, knew he wanted her badly. Why did it seem an eternity since they'd loved?

"Erin," he whispered. "I want you—"

The doorbell chimed, a dim sound that barely registered with her for a few seconds and then she twisted away. "Boone, that was the door. Someone's here—"

"They'll go away," he whispered.

"Boone! No one on this ranch is going to go away. It isn't a salesman peddling wares." She pushed away and wriggled into her dress and turned, holding up her hair. "Please zip me up."

"Damnation," he snapped, zipping her dress.

She turned around. "You see to it. I'll be right back," she said and hurried across the hall and into the formal living room.

"Erin, come back here, dammit. It's someone you probably know and I don't."

She ignored him, curious who would be at the door but wanting to get herself pulled together before she faced anyone she knew. She stepped in front of a mirror and looked at her flushed face, her red lips and disheveled hair. She pulled the clips out of her hair and combed it with one, dropping them both into her pocket while the door chimes rang again.

She wondered if Boone was trying to cool down and get

his shirt back into his slacks. She heard the door open and heard a deep male voice. When she recognized Uncle Perry's voice, she had to smother a laugh.

She had warned Boone about Hettie and Uncle Perry, and she would bet a great deal that Uncle Perry's unannounced appearance had something to do with Boone holding her hand and kissing her out in the yard in plain view of anyone who was in the vicinity.

She heard them talking but couldn't distinguish words.

Her amusement vanished as she thought about Boone and his wanting her to stay with him. That was the way to heart-break; she couldn't see it any other way. Yet if she told him no, he would probably pack and go out of her life almost as swiftly as he had come into it. And get rid of the Double T, as well.

Did she want to send away the most special man she had ever known without giving a relationship with him a chance? She knew she didn't want to lose the ranch, but she couldn't accept his proposition just to keep it.

Tormented and torn, she rubbed her forehead while most of her inclinations were to say yes to him.

She heard the door close. Tiptoeing to the door, she gazed into the empty hall and wondered where Boone had gone. When she looked out the window, she saw two of the men who worked on the ranch and guessed that Uncle Perry had brought some of the cowboys to the house to meet Boone.

Shaking her head, she went through the house to the kitchen where she found Boone had a table set and steaks ready. A tossed salad was in the refrigerator, potatoes were baking in the oven.

She saw the bottle of wine in a cooler on the counter. A scene set for seduction. The idea heated her and she longed to be back in his arms, but she knew she should take this quiet time to think things over and decide what she wanted tonight and for her future.

She went outside to sit on the patio. The patio had air-conditioning piped outside and it was enough to keep the area near the house cool. She thought about Boone's repeated statement that he wanted her. She knew he did, just as she wanted him, but it wasn't that simple. And all her willpower had turned to jelly in the past few minutes. She had meant it though, when she told him that he was rushing things.

It was thirty minutes later when he strode outside to join her. He shook his head. "You're not underage, are you?" he asked.

Smiling, she shook her head. "Hardly. I'm twenty-six. They wanted to meet you."

"Like hell. He wanted to keep me away from you. Will your uncle be back in about an hour? Or at ten o'clock? Or midnight?"

She shook her head. "No, he won't. He's being friendly. You'll see." She stood and headed toward the kitchen. "I'll help with dinner."

Boone caught her arm as his eyebrow arched. "Sit down. I'll bring drinks. What would you like? Wine, cocktail, pop, tea, beer?"

"Iced tea, please. I'll go with you to get it."

"I won't argue that one," he said, putting his arm around her and pulling her close against his side.

"Tell me more about your family," she said. "With all those brothers and sisters, which ones were you closest to?"

When they entered the kitchen, he released her to get her a glass of tea and a beer for himself. "I'm closest to my brother Zach. And I'm close to my sister Isabella."

"Isabella is next?"

"Nope," he said, carrying the tea and beer. "Let's sit outside, and I'll put dinner on shortly."

As they strolled back to the patio, he said, "My brother Ken is one year younger than I am—actually fifteen months younger. But Ken and I fought and he's irresponsible to this day and never did anything to help Mom—or me, for that matter."

"Where is he now?" she asked while Boone took her hand and led her to a cushioned glider. They sat close, and he put one arm behind her, wrapping his fingers lightly in her hair.

"Ken lives the life of a king in the mountains of Colorado. He married a wealthy woman who is a successful interior decorator and he helps her, I suppose. He doesn't have any other employment that I know of. Actually, I haven't seen him since Mom died four years ago, but that's what I'm told."

"So who's the next sibling?"

"Zach who's single and a navy SEAL."

"Another daredevil."

Boone shrugged. "I don't think either of us thought about our careers that way. I wanted to fly and to get away from home. Finding a way to do that in the military was a bonus." He paused to take a long drink of his beer.

Erin watched him, her pulse still skipping. Each brush of his fingers against her nape was electrifying and his kisses hadn't been long ago. In spite of trying to appear nonchalant about them, she was excited, fighting desire that burned in her like a banked fire.

His thick hair was temptation, and she wanted to comb her fingers through it as he was doing with hers. Instead, she sipped her iced tea and wished it would cool her down a degree.

"Where does Zach live?"

"The last I heard from him he was in Jordan, but that could have changed by this time."

"So where does Isabella fall in this line of siblings?"

"She's next. She's in California, dating a guy she wants me to come out and meet."

"So why don't you go?"

"I will," he said, smiling at her. "Don't sound so anxious to see me leave."

"I'm not. You just said you were close with her."

"I'm teasing. And I will go see her. Why don't you come with me and meet her?"

"We'll see," Erin replied, her pulse taking another leap at the thought of traveling with him. Anything with him played havoc with her pulse. "So, what does Isabella do?"

"She's a photographer. She was the first girl in our family and she became a little mother when the twins were born when she was two. She would help Mom in all sorts of ways, and we figured it was the female in her that made her want to play dolls with the new siblings. The rest of my siblings I'm not as close to and the youngest ones I really barely know. They were babies when I was a teen and trying to help support the family. A lot of the time I was gone or busy, and left their actual care to Isabella and Zach while I tried to earn some money."

"Do you have a picture?"

"No, I don't carry pictures of my siblings," he replied.

"Then tell me their names. After Isabella, who were the twins?"

"Vince and Jake, who are now twenty-five. Next Emily and Cathy and finally, Gregg who's twenty and in college at Texas University. Mom was pregnant with Gregg when Dad died. I left home after college at twenty-three."

"If you've been away that long, I'm surprised you're so opposed to marriage."

"I had twelve years of taking care of kids when I was growing up myself," he said quickly, remembering too many nights of walking a crying baby. "Dad was sick before he died, and Mom worked one job and tried to run the farm, and all of us who were old enough had to help with the farm. It was impossible and we moved away from there the next year.

"I was the oldest and was up at night with sick babies and had to coach my little brothers' soccer and had to take them with me hours on end. I've been a daddy and don't want that again. I don't want to marry and go through all that again," he said forcefully, and then looked at her. "I don't want to be tied down like I have been all of my life until I got into the military. I want freedom."

"Freedom might be lonely," she said.

"So far it hasn't been lonely," he replied and drew his fingers along her arm. "I used to dream of all the things I would do, places I would go. Frankly, marriage is prison."

"I don't think it would be prison with the right person," she said, thinking he had a cynical, harsh outlook on commitment. She knew she was forewarned. If she went into a relationship with him, it would not be lasting and he would never fall in love. "I think marriage with the right person would be the most wonderful thing possible."

"So why haven't you gotten out and dated more?"

"There's time for the right person to come along."

"You're a hopeless romantic."

"Maybe you're a hopeless cynic—except I don't think you are. You put your family first for years. There's some part of you deep down that likes a family."

"Well, it's pretty deep right now."

"You don't want children of your own?"

He shook his head. "I feel like I have children of my own. I'm sure you want a family."

"Yes, I do. As a matter of fact, I hope I have a big family. I think that would be wonderful. I love babies and little children."

"I'm sure you'll have that family, Erin," he said quietly and she knew it would never be with him.

"I'm sorry your mother didn't live long enough to enjoy your inheritance."

"I regret it, too," he said solemnly, and Erin reached up to give his wrist a squeeze. Instantly, his other hand covered hers and she gazed into his eyes that blazed with desire.

She placed her hand against his chest as he leaned toward her. "Just wait, Boone," she whispered, losing her voice and knowing she had no force in her statement at all.

He gave her a long, searching look and must have seen her sincerity because he sat back. "There are moments when I think you don't even like me, but then I remember last night and decide that you do."

"I like you!" she exclaimed, laughing at him. "I told you that you're going too fast for me."

"Give life a whirl, darlin'. You've been cooped up out here not really living for too long a time."

"I'm thinking about us, but I want to be sure before I let go again. I want to be sure of you."

"Oh, damn," he said softly, moving closer to her and wrapping an arm around her waist while the other was around her shoulders.

She placed her hand against his chest, feeling the steady beat of his heart.

"I am slowing to a crawl and about to disintegrate with wanting you."

"No one disintegrates from *that,* least of all you," she remarked, still struggling to hang on to her resolve. "You'll forget me as soon as you leave here."

"That's absolutely impossible," he told her solemnly.

As if he could read her mind, he placed his fingers along her throat and she realized that he was feeling her pulse. His eyebrows arched. "You're not quite as cool as you're acting," he said quietly in a huskier voice.

"Maybe not, but I meant what I said. Give me time and space."

"Sure thing, darlin'. But I don't know what's worrying you."

"Boone, how many women have you walked out on and left broken hearts behind? You can't tell me none. Not if you're truthful."

"I don't keep score, Erin. I can't tell you a number."

"I can imagine," she said dryly, standing up and picking up her iced tea. "Let's get dinner on to cook. I can help."

Disgruntled, Boone stood and caught up with her, keeping his hands to himself. All through grilling steaks and getting dinner on the table and over hot buttery rolls, thick, juicy steaks and fluffy, cheese-covered baked potatoes, he kept his hands to himself.

It wasn't until an hour after dinner that he slipped his arm around her waist and lifted her onto his lap while they sat on the glider on the patio. Only a few of the lights burned, leaving the patio in semidarkness.

He turned her to face him, reaching behind her to slide his fingers through her hair.

Erin wrapped her arms around his neck and pulled his head down to kiss him and his pulse soared.

Eventually, Erin ended their kisses as he had suspected she would. Boone raised his head. "Stop before you go too far to stop," she whispered.

"You're sure?" he asked, and her hand slipped down over his chest and she could feel his pounding heartbeat.

"Yes," she whispered. "For tonight, I'm positive."

"You won't stay with me?" he asked. "Ah, darlin', I need you." He sighed and shifted away, watching her as she sat up.

"Boone, there is no one woman you need or want that badly to settle down with." She straightened her clothing and turned to face him. "I should go home now."

"You misjudge me, darlin'."

"No, I don't think so," she replied.

He stood, draping his arm around her as they went through the house and across the yard to her house.

"Want a tour of my house?" she offered as they crossed her porch.

"Sure thing," he replied, taking her key and unlocking her door. Looking down at her with an arched eyebrow, he said, "If it were any other woman, I'd think you were asking me in to continue what we stopped. With you, I suspect it's to tour the house, but I'll do anything to stay with you longer."

"That's sweet."

"Erin, no one has ever accused me of being sweet," he said through clenched teeth.

She shrugged. "Seemed sweet to me. And my invitation really is to tour the house like I told you," she said. He stepped inside to hold the door for her.

"You have an alarm. You don't use it?" Boone demanded.

"Not unless I leave town. I feel safe here on the ranch."

"I suppose. There are so many treasures in that palace I've inherited, I probably should turn the alarm on, but it does seem needless out here."

"Those are your treasures now, Boone. You can take care of them however you want to. First on the tour of my home is the formal living room." She took his hand and he fell into step beside her.

"I'd rather have you back in my arms."

"Pay attention to my house. I like it."

"The least you can do is let me put my arm around you while I look."

She had him off balance tonight as much as she'd had him uncertain last night. To add to it, now he was uncertain about his future, yet the thought of packing and going back to Kansas City was totally unappealing. Last night he had seduced her, gotten her into his bed willingly and eagerly and had a wild, incredible night of passion.

He couldn't imagine that it wouldn't happen again, but he suspected he was going to have to dredge up patience, something he wasn't accustomed to doing and did not enjoy. He slid close to pull her against his side. She was warm, soft and sweet-smelling and he wondered how he could concentrate on her house or even notice it when all his attention was on her.

"The formal living room is not so formal," she said, leading him into a light, colorful room with a polished oak floor, white upholstered furniture with bright rainbow colors of pillows, potted plants and a varied collection of framed oils and watercolors on the walls.

"This looks like you," Boone said,

"Probably because I redecorated about five years ago. Now, the informal family room was my dad's."

She led Boone into a rustic room with wood everywhere: in the walls, ceilings, beams and floor. Maroon leather furniture looked as masculine as the antique rifle that hung over the mantel. A glass-fronted gun rack stood on one side of the room. Navaho rugs partially covered the oak floor. Western art decorated three walls while shelves with pictures and books lined another wall. One wall held a large brick fireplace and hearth.

The room and furnishings appealed to Boone, and he wondered about her father whom she seemed to have been close to. "I wish I could have known your dad," he remarked. "But then he probably would have viewed me in the same way Perry does and want to run me off the place."

"No such thing!" she replied. "And Uncle Perry doesn't want to run you off, either. Far from it. Neither Uncle Perry nor I want to see the ranch sold."

"I hope you're not spending time with me just for the ranch's sake," he said tersely.

"Of course not," she replied and gave him a smile.

Boone raised his brows, but remained silent.

"The rest are bedrooms and bathrooms and your usual standard bunch of rooms, including a games room and an exercise room and a few things like that."

"There's one room that's not a standard room and I'd like to see it so I know what to picture in my mind—your bedroom."

Six

"It's just a bedroom. You'll see it another time," she said, taking his hand and leading him down the hall, back the way they had come until they reached the front door, which she opened.

"I had a wonderful evening, Boone. And I do have to stop and think things over. You're moving way too fast."

Remaining inside, he shut the door to lean against it, pulling her closer with his hands on her waist. "Don't you want to talk a little longer? That's harmless."

"It's been a big day," she said, gazing at him solemnly, and Boone's disappointment grew.

She stood on tiptoe to kiss him on the cheek. Instantly his arm slipped around her waist and he turned his head to kiss her hard. He still leaned against the door and he pulled her up tightly against him, cupping her bottom, and then his hand tugged up her skirt and slipped beneath it, sliding over her bottom.

"Boone!" she gasped, twisting out of his grasp. His heart thudded when he saw the desire blazing in her green eyes.

"You want to love me, Erin."

"Of course I want to! But I want to wait and think about it."

He brushed a kiss on her cheek. "We have a dinner date tomorrow night if Perry doesn't do something to kill me in the morning."

"Uncle Perry will be friendly. There's nothing to worry about."

"Right," he remarked dryly. "Dinner about seven?"

"Yes. I had a wonderful time tonight," she whispered, and he clenched his fists to keep from reaching for her.

"Think about it, Erin. We're losing time we could have together. I really want you with me, darlin'. If I get back in time tomorrow, let's have lunch together."

"Fine," she replied as he stepped outside. She blew him a kiss and closed the door, leaning against it and closing her eyes. She ached for him, wanting him with a desperate need that tore at her, but his remarks about marriage had chilled her.

If she lived with him, she would be head over heels in love with him, if she wasn't already. And even if she was falling in love with him, if she lived with him for a time, it would be so much more difficult to separate.

And separate they would. His feelings on marriage were clear and forceful. When he had talked to her about his life, he had sounded angry and bitter. She ran her fingers across her forehead. Was she that old-fashioned that she couldn't forget the future and enjoy the present and then kiss him goodbye?

Her breath caught at the possibilities. Boone was excitement and sex and charm, so many things she had never really had in her life. A virile, handsome male who would keep her heart pounding and would be dazzling every day. And as a couple, they might last a long time.

For too long she had dreamed of a husband and children—a family like the one she had grown up in. Some of the happiest times she had ever experienced had been with her family, and she had always dreamed of having a family of her own. She sighed and knew she was hopelessly old-fashioned about a lot of things. She was tied to the ranch, she loved the horses and the job of managing the ranch, she did things the way her father had and her grandfather before him, wanting marriage and babies and a routine life on the ranch. Boone didn't fit into that picture in the least.

If she kept putting him off, she was certain he would pack and leave. The ranch held little interest for him. Therefore, she knew she should make some decisions quickly. Accept life with Boone on his terms and live with the consequences, or kiss him goodbye. Those were the choices. And if he left, he might sell the Double T. She hated to consider it but she knew she had to prepare for that possibility. She needed a plan.

Erin spent a sleepless night tossing and turning and wanting to be in Boone's arms. The next day she hardly saw him, and at four o'clock, the phone rang. Her pulse jumped at the sound of Boone's voice, but then she realized he sounded annoyed and impatient.

"Darlin', I'll be there for dinner when I can get there."

"That's fine, Boone," she replied. "Where are you?"

"Your uncle Perry wanted me to go to a horse sale with him. I'm in El Paso, Texas. We—"

She couldn't keep from laughing. "El Paso! How did you get to El Paso?"

"We flew down here in the ranch plane and he's found one thing after another to keep us here. I'm trying to get off on the right foot with him and be polite, but my patience is wearing thin. I want to have dinner with you."

"Do I have to tell him to bring you home?" she asked, trying to smother her laughter.

"Hell, no! I think we'll start back in about an hour, and I'm here to tell you, if he drums something up to keep me here past five o'clock, my cooperation is vanishing."

"Well, whenever you get here, give me a call. Dinner will wait."

"But I won't. I want to be with you. Does he do this with any guy who tries to date you, or is it just me?"

"I hate to tell you, but it's you. The few others years ago were locals and ranchers and I think, to Uncle Perry, that background made a difference. You're an outsider, and he may think your intentions are not honorable."

"They're damn sure not," Boone said, his voice softening. "I miss you something fierce."

"I miss you, too," she replied.

"Oh, damn. I feel like I'm a continent away from you. I'll hang up now and get this uncle of yours headed toward the airport. By the way, he bought a horse this afternoon, but if he thinks I'm coming back with him to pick it up, he's nuts."

"You don't have to be so polite to Uncle Perry."

"Yes, I do. He's sort of standing in for your father and I'm trying to please him."

"Good for you. Hurry home."

There was a pause and she heard him inhale. "That does it. See you about seven or a little after."

"Don't make rash promises. Just call when you get in."

"Sure. Soon, darlin'," he said and was gone. She replaced the receiver and smiled, but then her smile faded because she was back to her choices and knew she had to come to a decision. They were going dancing and Boone's patience had already worn thin. He would want an answer. She needed one herself.

* * *

By seven o'clock Erin was dressed in a slim, sleeveless black sheath. She had her hair looped and piled on her head and she wore the emerald cross necklace.

She glanced out the window and her bubbling eagerness mushroomed at the sight of Boone in a dark suit and tie, striding toward her house.

She grabbed her black envelope purse and hurried down to meet him, no longer caring how eager she looked. She flung open the front door just as he reached for the bell. The dark suit made him look handsome beyond all other times she had seen him. With his dashing dark looks, the navy suit and white shirt were breathtaking. Her desire raged into an uncontrollable bonfire.

She caught his wrist, half tugging him inside, but he came willingly, kicking the door closed behind him as he caught her up in his arms and kissed her hard.

She clung to him, kissing him back. Desire took her breath and built need for him. Unaware of pushing away his coat, she ignored his hands at her zipper until her dress fell away.

In seconds, clothing fell in dark puddles around their feet. Boone scooped her into his arms to carry her to the closest bedroom to place her on the bed. He came down beside her to wrap her in his arms while he kissed her and made love to her.

After a blinding consummation, he turned on his side, taking her with him. Holding her close, he showered kisses on her throat for seconds until he kissed her again, long and deeply, and she returned the kiss, letting all her desire for him go into her kiss, doing with kisses what she couldn't say with words.

Finally she raised her head to look him in the eyes. "You're a wild man, Boone Devlin. Now I have to bathe and dress again."

"Un-huh. Well, we'll do that little activity together, darlin'." He stared at her. Brilliant blue enveloped her as his gaze searched hers and conveyed his desire at the same time.

What was he thinking? she wondered, knowing she would never fathom most of his thoughts. He looked solemn, as if whatever was running through his mind was serious and something life-changing. She leaned down to kiss his neck, trailing kisses upward and breathing lightly into his ear.

"You'll start something all over again," he said gruffly, rolling away and picking her up. He looked around. "Let's get that bath. Give me directions to a bathroom."

"Put me down. My bedroom and bath are upstairs."

"I'm not putting you down yet," he said, shifting her in his arms to cradle her against his shoulder. "It's paradise to hold you in my arms and you're a feather. And you can't imagine what Perry had me hauling around today."

She leaned back to look at Boone. Excitement still bubbled fiercely in her and she tangled her fingers in his hair with one hand while she had the other arm wrapped around his neck. She couldn't touch him enough and she wasn't going to think about tomorrow yet.

He carried her upstairs easily, without being winded in the slightest. "My goodness, you're a strong one!" she gasped, running her hand over his biceps and then running her fingers along his chin. "I'm sorry about Uncle Perry, but I suspect you can protect yourself just fine."

"I told you, I don't want to get on the wrong side of him. He's as close as it comes to dealing with your father, and I feel like I need to earn his friendship and respect, so I'm not going to blow him off."

"This is a side of my uncle that I've never seen, but then I've never dated an outsider and I've actually dated very little, all things considered."

"Something I still find difficult to believe except for the fact that you're out here in the boonies where no one can find you except the local cowboys and, thankfully, they haven't impressed you."

"You've got a bruise on your jaw that I don't recall you having last night," she said, studying him.

"Could be. Perry's not the only one on this ranch who would like to see me pack and go."

"No kidding? What did the guys do to you?"

Boone grinned. "They had some horse saddled this morning, and when I met Perry and we went to mount up—"

"Wait a minute. Why were you riding?" she asked. "Perry always goes in a truck. He doesn't ride a horse to get anywhere on this ranch."

"He said where we were going was rugged ground because he thought I'd want to see the entire ranch, so we'd go on horseback."

She groaned. "Am *I* going to have to protect you from those guys?"

"No, you're not."

"The room at the end of the hall is my bedroom," she directed.

He entered a room in pink with green accents and was momentarily startled, pausing to look around, his gaze resting on her four-poster bed. "This surprises me. It doesn't exactly look like you."

"I like pink, but I'm a redhead and don't wear it very much."

"Well, it's all very female looking."

She smiled up at him. "You are the first man to be in it outside of relatives."

He nodded, looking into her eyes. "I'm glad. I can't believe my luck."

"Oh, come now. None of that. The bathroom is through that door."

He entered a pink bathroom and grinned. "Pink tub, pink walls, I'm going to drown in pink in here."

"As a matter of fact, I think you'll be fine. Put me down."

With a grin Boone set her on her feet and her gaze drifted over him as she ran her hands over his bare chest. "Mmm, do you look fantastic in pink!"

He laughed while she watched him move around, and in minutes she was sitting between his legs in hot bubbly water. As she pinned up her hair, he sponged off her back.

"Now, finish telling me about your day," she said. "You met Perry early this morning and you rode horseback to look at the ranch."

"He asked me if I'd ever ridden and I said I had. The guys saddled horses for us while Perry met me. When we got to the horses, Perry took one look at my horse and started cussing and asking who'd saddled the horse and told some guy to get me another one."

"Did you have a leggy roan with floppy ears and a Roman nose?" she asked, twisting around to look at him. Boone nuzzled her neck, trailing his tongue to her ear, and she inhaled, desire ignited a curling flame deep inside.

"Yep, that's the one."

"That's dreadful, Boone! That's Tornado. He's farmed out to local rodeos and he's mean and he's impossible and no one rides him."

"Well, guess what—"

"You don't have to prove anything to those guys." She twisted around farther to look at him. "You were in Special Forces, for heaven's sake!" she said, aghast at the welcome he was getting from men who were like family to her.

"Oh, yes I do."

"Men and their macho egos! Boone, really—"

"Oh, no, missy. It's because of you. Otherwise, they could all go fly a kite. No, I got on that beast and rode him and managed to stick on. They were good-natured about it and brought me another horse, but—and this was the dumb move on my part—I said that I'd just ride the roan. To Perry's credit, he tried to discourage me."

"That *was* a poor decision," she agreed, turning her back to him again and leaning against him, rubbing her foot along his leg slowly.

"Well, we did pretty well for an hour, and then when I let down my guard, the horse tossed me into a bunch of bushes."

"Poor baby," she said, twisting around again to kiss Boone's jaw, trailing kisses to his throat once more.

"If this is what I get for being thrown into the briar patch, it was worth it," he drawled. "I rode him home after that and think I gained a little friendship out of those guys for sticking with that mangy beast."

"Tornado isn't mangy, but he is a beast. And I'm sure you did earn respect and friendship, but you own this place. I can't believe that they did that to you! They'll respect you for riding Tornado, though. I need to have a talk with Perry."

"No you don't, darlin'. Don't interfere here. This is a man thing and they're just looking out for you. Their intentions are good, even if their behavior is damn annoying. Toting me off to El Paso today was mean, and I don't think I would have gotten here when I did except I told Perry that I was leaving him there. I said I would fly back on my own, so he gave up and came with me."

She turned and wrapped her arm around Boone's neck. "I'm glad you did," she said in a sultry voice, and his eyes narrowed. His arms wrapped around her and he caught her up tightly against him while he kissed her.

He cupped her breast and she felt his arousal. He was warm and wet and she slid her hands over his sculpted chest, caressing hard muscles and sliding down over his flat, washboard stomach.

Splashing water over the tub and onto the floor, he stood and pulled her up, picking her up to step out of the tub. "Erin, darlin', I need you," he whispered as he showered kisses down her throat and then cupped her breasts to circle one nipple with his thumb while he bent and took her other nipple into his mouth. His tongue flicked over her nipple and she gasped with pleasure, running her hands over his powerful shoulders, finally kneeling on the soft bathroom rug. She stroked him, sliding her tongue the length of his manhood as she caressed him and then took him into her mouth to kiss and tease him as he had her.

He plunged his fingers into her hair and she heard his groan and then her name.

"Erin, ah, Erin, love…" His voice trailed away and she knew the words were simply spoken in the throes of passion and meaningless endearments to him that he probably didn't even know he was saying.

By the time he scooped her into his arms and carried her into her bedroom, they were both dry, their bodies heated from lovemaking.

Standing her on her feet, he flung back the covers and turned to take her into his arms and kiss her. She was barely aware when he picked her up and placed her on the bed, moving between her legs. He knelt to trail kisses along the inside of her thigh and she arched her hips, crying out as he kissed her intimately, driving her to a consuming urgency. He leaned over to retrieve a packet from the table. As soon as he put it on, he took her in his arms.

"Boone!" she cried, pulling him to her.

He entered her slowly and withdrew and she tried to hold

him, her legs tightening around him while she ran her hands down his back to cup his firm, narrow buttocks.

"Love me," she cried, and then his mouth covered hers and her cries were muffled as she arched against him.

He continued moving slowly, filling her while driving her to a frenzy of need. Sweat dotted his forehead and shoulders as he struggled to maintain control.

Her pulse roared and she was unaware of anything except the sensations storming her, driving her to the brink.

Then he lost control and they both moved wildly and a culmination rocked her, spasms rippling through both of them until he lowered his weight on her and she wrapped her arms around him to hold him tightly while they kissed.

Their ragged breathing and pounding heartbeats slowed eventually and became steady and regular. She stroked his back lightly while she combed her fingers through his hair and he showered her with light kisses.

"Erin, darlin', you're magic!" he whispered. "I've dreamed of you, wanted you, longed for you. Each day I'm going crazy thinking about you."

"I hope so," she said softly in return. "It's mutual, Boone. This is a first in my life in so many ways."

"Have you thought anymore about staying with me?"

"Of course I have. It's a big step and I still haven't decided. We haven't known each other a week yet."

"We've known about each other longer than that."

She smiled as she trailed her fingers along his jaw. "You mean I've known about *you* a lot longer. I've been hearing about the dashing and brave and brilliant Boone Devlin, Jonah Whitewolf and Mike Remington—and Colin Garrick—for a long time. You haven't heard anything about *me* except my name and that I manage the ranch."

"Erin, it won't be a casual relationship," he said with such solemnity she caught his face to gaze into his eyes. He gave her a steadfast look in return and she wished she could count on him really meaning what he said, but his attitude about marriage haunted her.

"I'm thinking, Boone. In the meantime, do we get to eat tonight?"

"How can you think about food?" he asked, his eyes twinkling. "Maybe I can get that notion out of your head," he whispered, nuzzling her neck and then tickling her with his stubble of whiskers.

Laughing, she pushed lightly against him. "It won't work. I have to eat. Did you and Perry eat on the way back?"

"No. I haven't had anything since lunch today and that was a burger at a drive-through on the way to the airport and left a lot to be desired." He rolled over and stood, reaching down to pick her up.

"C'mon, woman, and we'll shower and then go eat."

"Just remember—you promised we would eat," she teased, knowing if they showered together, they would both be tempted to forget eating dinner.

In another half hour she was wrapped in a blue silk robe and he wore only his jeans as they sat on her patio and ate steaks that Boone had grilled.

Her Olympic-size pool sparkled and a cool breeze wafted across the patio, but Erin was only aware of Boone.

"You missed getting to go dancing tonight," he said, leaning back with a cold beer in his hand while he talked to her.

"We can do that another time," she answered easily.

"You've turned my life upside down," he said.

She shook her head. "Wrong. I'm the one whose life is topsy-turvy and will never be the same."

He set down the beer and reached over to catch her wrist. "Come sit in my lap."

She moved over to sit on his lap and wrap her arms around his neck. He wrapped one arm around her waist while he moved his other hand along her knee, pushing open her silk robe.

"Erin, if I put the ranch on the market, what will you do?"

His question chilled her and she raised her head to look at him. "I've thought about it some. I've meant to talk to Uncle Perry. Maybe the two of us could buy the Double T—I have to talk to my banker, too. Have you decided to sell?"

"I want you to be happy," he said.

"And if I don't agree to your selling it—then what?"

"Then I guess I'll have to keep the place," he said, kissing her lightly, brushing a kiss on her ear. She tingled, but at the same time, worry plagued her because his question increased her concern about the future of the ranch. If she flatly refused, they would be at an impasse, but it would be an unpleasant one.

"We don't have to worry about it now because I'm not going anywhere very far from you anytime soon."

While he brushed light kisses on her mouth and her concerns over the ranch diminished with each seductive kiss.

"I can't think about anything else for more than ten seconds without you getting into my thoughts and ruining my concentration," he whispered.

She pulled his head forward to kiss him and before the hour was up, he carried her to the chaise to make love to her.

It was before dawn when they were back in her bed that Erin shook him awake. "Boone!"

He sat up, instantly stepping out of bed. "What?"

She gasped in surprise at how fast he had awakened. "I didn't mean to startle you. I just wanted you to wake up."

"Oh, darlin'," he said, crawling back into bed to pull her into his arms. She pushed against his chest.

"Wait a minute! I wanted you to wake up and go home."

He raised on one elbow. "Why?"

She was glad it was semidark in the bedroom, with only a small light in the bathroom burning, because she felt a blush heat her face. "I don't want you to cross paths with Uncle Perry as you go home. Or with Hettie. I'm sorry, but you've entangled yourself with a very old-fashioned woman—"

"But adorable," he said, interrupting her with a long kiss. Then he stopped and rolled away to get up. "I will shower alone and be gone before either one of the fire-breathing dragons who guard you come after me or even know that I've been here."

"I know both of them will know you've been here, but I just hope they don't know exactly when you leave here."

She watched him gather his clothes and stride toward the bathroom. Her gaze ran down his muscled back, down over his firm buttocks and long legs that were sprinkled with short, dark hair.

The night hadn't gone as she had intended, and there were problems and questions to face all too soon, but for a few hours, they had captured the joy of loving each other and during that time, everything else was suspended.

At the door downstairs, as he kissed her goodbye and she stepped away, she caught his hand.

"Boone, give some thought to keeping the ranch and just enjoying it and taking the profits from it. Will you do that?" she asked him.

"Sure thing, darlin'," he replied, kissing her lightly. "Stop worrying about it. I won't do anything to hurt you."

Turning, he strode away, finally disappearing in the shadows and then reappearing in his own yard. She stood until he reached his door. He turned and waved and she waved back before going inside and locking up.

She closed the door and walked back to bed without thinking about what she was doing. She couldn't imagine him coming back to vacation—unless she was in his bed when he did. As much as she was attracted to him, she was just too old-fashioned to accept his casual ways. And she didn't think he would stay long at the Double T. She was going to have to give him an answer about moving in with him and she knew she might as well go ahead and do it when she saw him tomorrow.

She rubbed her forehead. That was one problem between them. A bigger one was the future of the ranch.

What if she said no to his selling the ranch? Could she really stop him since he had full ownership? She made a mental note to call Savannah Remington as soon as possible.

She needed to talk to Savannah about her rights involving the ranch. It was really Boone's ranch now and if he wanted to sell it, she didn't think she could stop him, but maybe the will was totally binding.

A terrible feeling curled in the pit of her stomach. Why did the sexiest, most handsome man she had ever met also have to be the man who might wreck her life and take the thing she loved most away from her?

Seven

Erin slept little and Saturday she dressed in a T-shirt and cutoffs. She was eager to see Boone while at the same time, she dreaded what she knew they had to discuss.

She didn't think he would have one more thing to say about selling the ranch today than he'd had last night. He wasn't in a hurry and for that, she didn't know whether to be glad or not, because the future of the ranch was a constant concern.

Erin knocked on Boone's kitchen door and he glanced out to see her, wind catching her hair. He crossed the kitchen, and her eagerness won out over her worry as he threw open the kitchen door and she walked into his arms.

She stepped into the kitchen and kicked the door closed while he kissed her.

When Erin pushed against his chest, Boone raised his head. Dazed, he looked down at her. Her solemn expression gave him a hint what was coming and he braced for bad news.

"Boone, I won't move in with you yet."

He hurt, wanting her, yet not surprised and not totally daunted.

"But we'll still see each other?" he asked, holding his breath. This was the one woman who had him unable to guess the next move. Always before, the women in his life had been predictable, but there was nothing predictable about Erin.

She nodded solemnly and he let out his breath, kissing her lightly. "Then I'm happy," he said. "Could be happier, but if we can keep on seeing each other like we do now, I'll settle for that and be happy. You might change your mind," he offered playfully, but he meant it and watched her reaction.

Again, she nodded, seeming to think over what he'd said. "I might. I know you consider me hopelessly old-fashioned, but I think you're rushing into things. You're not going to change, so it's up to me to slow this down."

He nuzzled her throat. "Fine with me. If you'll spend time with me, then we'll just go from there."

"Good. And it's still early in the evening. Why don't we get dressed and I'll show you a place to go dancing. It's sort of a honky-tonk so we'll go in jeans."

"Whatever you want," he said, tightening his arms around her to kiss her. He turned her against his shoulder, leaning over her, and she wrapped her arms around his neck, and by the time the subject of dancing came up again, it was far too late in the night to go.

"I should go home now," Erin said, slipping out of bed and gathering up her things to hurry to the shower.

When she came out, Boone had showered and dressed, his dark hair still wet and combed sleekly back, giving him a dangerous, rougher look, yet still handsome enough to take her breath.

"I'll walk you home," he said, taking her hand as they went through the house.

"Tomorrow's Sunday. You want to go to church with me in Stallion Pass and meet people there?"

"Sure. I'll do anything with you that you'd like to do."

Erin glanced up at him, thinking that there was one thing he wouldn't do with her—marriage. The more she was with him, the more his attitude about marriage bothered her because she knew that was what she wanted in life. No temporary affair for her, yet she realized she was already into a temporary one.

"So what time is church? Some early hour like Perry hauling me out before sunrise?"

She laughed. "You're going to have to stand up to Uncle Perry at some point. I would never have guessed what a marshmallow you would be with those guys."

"Just for you, darlin'," he replied. "Like I told you, I want to stay on Perry's good side if I can. And he stayed out of my hair today."

"Next week may be another story. You don't have to involve yourself with the ranch."

"Might as well. While I'm here, I want to know about it. Perry won't run me off, and we'll get a decent relationship established."

"You don't want me to talk to him?"

"You do and you're in trouble. I can take care of myself with Perry and the rest of them. Even Tornado—he tossed me once, but I spent the rest of the day riding him. Maybe he'll be my horse."

She laughed as they crossed her porch and he swung her into his embrace. "Ah, Erin. What you do to my heartbeat! Let me come in for a short time."

She shook her head while she wrapped her arms around

his neck and stood on tiptoe. "Not tonight. Sorry, Boone, but I can't." She kissed him before he could protest and he tightened his arms, kissing her long and passionately until she pushed against his chest.

"Night, Boone," she said softly and unlocked her door, stepping inside. "See you in the morning about seven."

She closed the door in his face and he stared at it.

He realized he was standing, staring at a door, so he turned, crossed the porch and strode across her yard. Unaware of what he was doing, he vaulted the fence instead of opening the gate. He wanted her in his arms and thought about moving to Texas.

He ought to leave and go back to Kansas City, but he wanted to stay close to Erin.

He raked his fingers through his hair and laughed at himself. When had he ever been concerned that a woman might not be interested in him? Not since he was about fifteen.

He would go to Kansas City, soon.

He swam and worked out and did everything he could think of to wear himself down so he would sleep.

As Boone ran on an indoor track in the exercise room, he continued to think about Erin. He knew she wanted commitment, probably marriage, but he had made it clear that he couldn't marry. That was out and she had known that from the first and still been willing to make love and see each other, so it might just be a matter of time until she moved in with him. She always talked about him rushing to get what he wanted and he had to admit that she was right.

Lost in memories of making love to her, he groaned. He knew he had to stop thinking about her every second when he wasn't with her.

The feisty redhead did have him tied in knots. He made a mental note to go to a jeweler's and get something special for her.

By four in the morning he tossed aside the sheet and sat up, running his hand through his hair and wondering why he couldn't get her out of his thoughts. He reached for the phone and called her, his pulse jumping when he heard her sleep-filled voice. He could imagine her warm and tousled, lying in bed, and he became aroused.

"Boone? What? It's 4:00 a.m.! Are you all right?" she asked, alarm filling her voice as she became more awake.

"I'm fine except I miss you."

"For heaven's sake! Go to bed!" She hung up the receiver, and he stared in consternation at the phone.

"Dammit, Erin," he said, tempted to call her again, but she would just hang up again. When had that ever happened to him before? He had to laugh at himself. "You're still a pompous jackass," he told himself aloud in the dark bedroom and got up to go swim, hoping to exhaust himself before the sun came up.

Finally, it was almost dawn when he sprawled across his bed and slept, only to wake to the alarm and have to hurry to get to Erin's in time to go to church.

He showered, shaved and dressed in a brown suit, going to get Erin. At the sight of her in a sleeveless turquoise dress, he wanted to toss aside plans for the day and take her into his arms, but he knew she would say no.

Beneath a bright, sunny sky, they went to Erin's church in Stallion Pass and then to eat at the Stallion Pass Country Club. Boone left the car with a valet and took Erin's arm.

As they headed toward the door, Boone saw a familiar head of black hair and recognized his friend Mike Remington and Mike's blond wife, Savannah. Boone shook hands with his tall friend while the Remingtons greeted Erin, whom they already knew. Erin and Boone spoke to Jessie, the baby girl Mike held in his arms. Jessie gazed at them with big blue eyes, her face framed by a pink bonnet.

As the women chatted and played with the baby, Mike glanced at Erin and then back at Boone. "How's the sale of the ranch coming along?"

"I'm in no rush. I'm living there."

"That was quick, but she's a beauty," Mike said in a low voice.

"I'm learning about the ranch." Boone said.

"You don't know a thing about quarter horses," Mike remarked dryly.

"Doesn't matter. I'll sell the Double T in time."

"I might have an acquaintance who would be interested in the ranch," Mike offered. "If I need to get in touch with you, I have your cell number. Otherwise, do I call your house or hers?"

"Call mine if you want me. Call hers if you want her."

Mike's eyebrows rose higher, and his eyes twinkled as he glanced at Erin again and then back at Boone. "If she's not living in your house, this is a first. Women fall for you like you're the only man left on earth. You've found one who doesn't hang on your every word and give in to your every whim?"

"I guess you could put it that way," Boone snapped, and Mike grinned.

"I never thought I'd see the day! Much less with the manager of the horse ranch. I made a bet with Savannah. When she told me about Erin's age, we made a bet that Erin would succumb to your charms within twenty-four hours. I take it that I've lost that bet completely."

"Yes, you have. How's your security business?"

"You're changing the subject and you're getting prickly. I'm beginning to be impressed with Miss Frye. I hardly know her, but we'll have to have you two over for dinner sometime soon."

"I suppose I deserve this," Boone admitted. "Who's the best jeweler around here?"

"For a wedding ring or—"

"Oh, hell, no wedding ring! I'm not *marrying* anyone. This is just a new experience with Erin. I *haven't* changed. I'm *not* about to get locked up in marriage vows."

"Is that right? Well, there are three jewelry stores on Main, and you can't go wrong with any of them, but I like J. Danforth's the best."

"Thank you," Boone said, knowing Mike was still laughing at him and having to admit that he probably did deserve it because in the past women had always been easy.

He glanced at Erin, his gaze skimming over her in her tailored turquoise dress. She looked beautiful, proper, cool. But he wasn't so wrapped up that he was thinking about marriage. That *wasn't* going to happen.

Moving closer to Erin, he slipped his arm around her waist. They talked a few more minutes to the Remingtons and then parted from the couple. Boone and Erin entered the clubhouse.

"Have you known Savannah long?" he asked Erin.

"All my life. We're both from this area. We've never been close, but we're friends and since she was John's attorney, we've had business dealings because of the ranch and wills and inheritances. That sort of stuff."

They crossed the polished hardwood floor of the large foyer and entered the dining room where they were seated by a window with a view of the golf course. A bouquet of daisies was a cheerful contrast to the forest-green, linen tablecloth.

Over grilled Alaskan salmon, they talked about the week ahead, a week that was coming up too quickly to suit Boone. He wasn't ready to go back to Kansas City yet, but he knew business was piling up and there were transactions only he could authorize. Reluctantly, he knew he had to tell Erin.

"I'll fly back to Kansas City Monday morning."

"Fine," she said, sipping her water. "Will you come back soon?"

"Probably," he said, knowing he was being indefinite, but he had never liked being pinned down or having to make definite commitments and he wasn't ready to start now.

"I'll take you to the airport," she said and he nodded, seeing a little cloud of worry in her eyes and wondering how much she cared what he did.

He needed to fly home for business, and he wanted a breather. Erin dazzled him and he wanted to get away and see her in perspective and cool down a little. This whole affair with her was so unlike any he had ever had with another woman.

At the same time, he wanted to make love to her before he left town. If he had his way, they would have a whole night of loving, but she might say no to that one.

After they ate, they drove back to the Double T, deciding to go for a swim as soon as they reached the ranch.

When they reached the border to the ranch, he glanced at the fence. "Erin, that old wood fence is picturesque, but when I've been out in a truck and looked at it closely, it's rotten in places. Have you ever thought about replacing it with pipe fencing?"

"No, I haven't," she answered coolly and in a glance he saw she was bristling at the suggestion. "We can repair or replace it where it's rotted away. That's what we've been doing."

"That's a damned expensive way to take care of it."

"We can afford to mend the fences."

"How old is most of that fence?"

"It's old, but sturdy," she answered in what he thought was

an evasive manner. He knew if he got a buyer for the ranch, the outdated fences would be a drawback to a sale.

"Your fences are ancient and dilapidated and falling down in spots. It would be cost efficient, not to mention being stronger, to replace them."

"You don't know that much about ranching or this ranch in particular. We're not changing the fences. They add to our charm."

"There's charm here, all right, and the prettiest smile in Texas," he said, catching her hand and placing it on his thigh and the fence conversation was dropped.

The next morning on Monday, Boone stopped by Erin's house at seven to tell her goodbye as he left for Kansas City. She stood in the window, watching him drive away, and had a pang of loss, which she told herself was ridiculous.

She wanted to stay with him, but she knew she shouldn't. She was falling in love with him, there was no escaping that fact, but she tried to keep it hidden from him so he wouldn't feel guilty about not loving in return. Was it real—a true love that would last? Or was it infatuation? The answers eluded her now. Time would hold the only answers.

She shook her head and turned away to go to work catching up on bookkeeping and calls and myriad things she had put off because of Boone.

During the day he called her half a dozen times, and that night while she lay in bed, she talked for three hours with him.

She replaced the receiver, smiling. She fell asleep mulling over her future and what she wanted to do, missing him and their times together. She longed for his arms around her tonight. She wanted his arms around her every night. It would be so easy, so wonderful to stay with him. To pretend this would last forever. She wasn't one to rush into things, especially not when that seemed the road to heartbreak.

Was she really holding out for a marriage proposal?

She had to admit that she might be. She knew she'd never get that from Boone, but that's what she had always wanted with the man she loved. It couldn't be a casual thing the way Boone wanted it to be.

She wanted to know about Boone's family. He barely mentioned them. He had answered her questions about them, but otherwise, he didn't talk about them.

She sighed and rubbed her forehead. Why did he have to be so special to her? But he was special, incredibly so.

As the days passed while he was in Kansas City, they talked often on the phone, but the night calls lasted hours. Thursday night when he called, he told her he could not get away as easily as he had expected and he would have to stay into the next week.

When he returned to the ranch, she was waiting on the porch. She had rehearsed what she would say and do, wanting to resist falling into his arms and have some restraint from the start—more than she had shown the night she met him. Instead, when he stepped out of a black car and slammed the door, her heart thudded against her ribs and she could not keep from dashing down the steps and running to meet him.

He caught her up in his arms and kissed her senseless. She felt as if she were melting into a quivering heap and she returned his kisses passionately. She held his strong shoulders, clinging to him until he picked her up and carried her inside the house and kicked the door shut and then clothes were shed in haste.

Her pulse was like rolling thunder, and her heart pounded. She couldn't get enough of him. His warm, bare body was magnificent and she had missed him, missed his loving beyond anything she had imagined possible.

"I'm glad you're back," she whispered.

"So am I, darlin'," he answered, showering kisses on her.

In minutes he had on protection and picked her up to slide her down on his hard shaft. Their hips danced in an ancient rhythm until they were carried to the heights and release poured over her at the same time she knew it did Boone.

She was draped over him, holding him tightly while her heartbeat and breathing returned to normal. "I missed you," she said.

"Ah, I missed you and being here and I'm damn glad to be back," Boone said.

"This seems so right, Boone," she whispered, but she didn't get an answer.

"Let's find a bed before I melt and slide down in a puddle at your feet," he said, setting her on her feet. She scooped up her clothes as he grabbed his and they went to his bathroom to shower before they got into his big bed. He pulled her close.

"Welcome home," she said softly, drawing her fingers along his jaw.

"That was the best welcome ever," he said and brushed a kiss on her temple. "Am I glad to be here!"

"I was going to show a little restraint, but somehow that just vanishes when I'm with you."

He chuckled. "I hope so," he drawled. "I'm glad to be back."

"How long will you stay this time?"

"You want me to stay?"

"Of course, I do," she answered and he pulled her close to kiss her.

They talked for hours, ate, made love and talked through

the night. She had an endless store of events to tell him about and wanted to hear all about his time in Kansas City.

It was almost four in the morning before she fell asleep in his arms. In all their talking, Boone had never answered her question about how long he would stay at the Double T this time.

The next day he went back out with her uncle and the cowboys and fell into a routine at the ranch that surprised her.

During the next week, she saw her uncle briefly one morning when he came by the house to talk to her about a rancher who was interested in a particular horse. As he pocketed a card she had given him, he turned before he crossed the porch.

"Boone is taking a real interest in this ranch," Perry said, pushing his hat back on his head.

"I'm surprised," she replied, leaning one hip against the doorjamb.

"So am I, Erin. He's sharp and quick, but then John Frates told me that about him. John said if anything ever happened and Boone got the ranch, we'd be all right and maybe better than we had been under the Frateses' guidance."

"I can't imagine that happening."

"Nope, I haven't seen that yet, but Devlin is a fast learner. And he takes to horses as if he grew up here. Are you happy with him, honey?" Perry asked, and she knew he worried about her, but the words went deep.

"Yes, I am. Don't worry, Uncle Perry. I can take care of myself."

"When it comes to matters of the heart, Erin, none of us can take care of ourselves. I'd sure be letting your daddy down if I stood by and you got hurt badly."

"I'm all right," she said, smiling at him. Later, she was to remember that moment, and even at the time, she felt a strange little frisson shake her and make her wonder if she was tempting fate.

* * *

That night when she ate dinner with Boone, the two of them sat on the cool patio at his house and she thought about Boone and the horses. "You're not still riding Tornado, are you?" she asked, looking at Boone's thick, long lashes, his sexy blue eyes. He was wearing jeans with a light blue knit shirt that made his eyes seem even more blue.

"Yes, I am. None of you understand that maverick," he said, lightly caressing her nape as they sat on the glider together. Boone pushed lightly with his toe, causing the glider to swing back and forth gently, but the motion bothered Erin slightly.

"And *you* do?" she asked with amusement. His caresses were stirring up a storm in her that she was trying to ignore.

"Yep. *I'm* the one riding him, aren't I, when no one else could."

"You've got a point. But as Uncle Perry said, someday that horse will toss you into tomorrow and then you'll feel differently about it."

"We'll see," Boone said, moving closer to her and winding her fingers with his. He brushed light kisses across her knuckles, and then reached up to trace his finger along her throat.

"You look great," he said softly, smiling at her.

"I'm just wearing cutoffs and a blouse—pretty simple stuff," she said, thinking he was the one who looked great.

"Cutoffs, whatever, you take my breath, darlin'."

"I hear you are really getting into the ranching business. My uncle says you're a fast learner."

"I like the Double T, but then there's a special reason I like it here. And speaking of the ranch, darlin', those stables are a firetrap. There's plenty of money to replace them with—"

"Whoa!" she said, annoyance her first reaction. "Those stables are a tradition, and we have a modern sprinkler system."

"It may be modern, but it's damn inadequate, and like I said, the stables are a firetrap."

"Boone, are you going to come in here and start changing things?" she said, knowing she was sounding sharp and that she was glaring at him, but her anger was rising.

"Only if I feel they really need changing badly," he answered calmly. "I think the stables are a hazard for everyone on the ranch and for any horses kept in them."

"You're an outsider," she said, her annoyance increasing.

"That's why I can view it without sentimentality," he answered with exasperating patience that was a switch for him.

"Those stables are steeped in tradition! With the sprinkler system, they're well protected. Do you know how many years they've been standing, and we've never once had a fire?"

"What was it? One hundred and thirty-nine years, right?" he replied, and she was astounded that he remembered.

"Doesn't mean it can't happen," he added.

"I'll fight you on this," she said, her anger growing. "You've been here three weeks and you want to change things. I love those stables, and they're part of the charm and heritage of the Double T. They're as safe as new ones would be. John was satisfied with them."

"Erin, you're thinking with your heart and not your head," he said with such patience she wanted to scream. This man who had never shown a shred of patience before was suddenly talking to her as if he were explaining a situation to a stubborn child.

"Keep one building for sentiment and let's update and replace the other two and use them. You'll still have your old barn to look quaint and charming and you'll have two safe, state-of-the-art new ones."

"What we have is state-of-the-art enough," she said evenly. "We're not replacing even one building."

"Now, aren't you being a little stubborn?" he asked with an arch of his eyebrow.

"Stop patronizing me! Maybe I'm being stubborn, but it's for an excellent reason. Those stables *are* safe. They're picturesque, and they're featured in our brochures and have appeared in national magazines. No, we're not tearing them down."

He shook his head. "You're seeing them through proverbial rose-colored glasses. Look again, Erin. They are a real worn-out, outdated firetrap. Perry is noncommittal because he knows you love them."

"He's noncommittal because he doesn't agree with you," she snapped. Agitated, her stomach churning, she wanted off the glider and to put some space between Boone and her.

Abruptly, she stood and moved away, walking across the patio to gaze into the darkness, seeing the wooden stables in her mind's eye. "Those stables are fine. I *know* they are," she said, turning to face Boone. He sat on the glider, his arm across the back and his long legs stretched out in front of him, crossed at the ankles. He looked relaxed, confident and undisturbed.

"You get a fireman to check out the sprinkler system with you and see what he says," she said.

"I did," Boone replied quietly, surprising her. Standing, he crossed to her to put his hands on her shoulders. "Stallion Pass Chief Wardell agrees with me."

"I don't believe you," she started, took one look in his eyes and inhaled. "All right, so he does. That doesn't mean he's right, either. I'm going to go look at them right now."

"Fine," Boone said, sliding his arm across her shoulders.

She shrugged him away. "By myself," she snapped. "I want to look around. I'll call you later."

He placed his hands on his hips and smiled slightly at her. "You're getting angry over something we can work out sensibly."

"There is nothing to work out, Boone. We're not replacing the stables when there is no reason to."

"You go look at them, darlin'. And try to keep an open mind when you do. You think about the safety of those horses you love. Think about your own horse in that stable during a nasty lightning storm."

"We have lightning rods."

"That's not an absolute and you know it, Erin."

He walked her to the front gate. "Sure you don't want me to come? It's late."

"No. I want to look at them by myself."

"Don't go away angry over some old stables, darlin'. Come here." Boone wrapped his arms around her, and the moment she was in his embrace, it was difficult for her to think about stables or anything except the handsome man holding her.

He was strong and lean and marvelous to touch. His mouth covered hers and his tongue stroked hers. Heat pooled in her and became an ache low inside. She wanted to love him all night, and she fought all her inclinations even though she kissed him back and rubbed her hips against his.

His hand slipped beneath her shirt to caress her breast and then he circled her taut nipple.

"Boone!" she gasped, pleasure and desire streaking in her. He was aroused, ready and she was hot, wanting him.

She had no idea how much time passed, but he leaned away. "Come back inside with me?" he invited in a husky, coaxing voice. Torn between wanting him and worrying about the ranch, she shook her head.

"No, I still want to look at the stables tonight."

"They'll be there tomorrow."

"*Tonight,* Boone. And *alone,*" she said, stepping out of his arms.

He watched her walk away, in that sexy walk she had. Her long shapely legs were bare, the cutoffs hugging her trim bottom. He wanted her more every hour—was he falling in love with her?

Instantly he rejected the notion as ridiculous, but then he thought about it again. He wouldn't know real love if it jumped up and bit him. He didn't think this was a once-and-forever deal, yet he had to admit she had him tangled into sleeplessness, longing and need that he had never experienced before in his life.

"Darlin', what are you doing to me?" he whispered, watching her and trailing after her. Love—something he had never associated with himself. And he still didn't. He shook his head, looking at her as he crossed the driveway and headed toward the stables. With the myriad night-lights in most of the surrounding area, it was as bright as day. Boone knew she was safe, but he didn't like her wandering around alone at night. He waited until she disappeared inside a stable and then he moved out of the perimeter of light where he could be within close distance if she did need someone.

What were the depths of his feelings for her? Was he falling in love? Love was something that happened to other people, marriage-minded people. Not Boone Devlin. He realized he better think about what that would mean.

Tonight, he had angered her. He just hoped she could see his reasoning before it was too late. And that it wouldn't put a wedge between them.

Erin stood in the empty stable, fuming as she looked up at the shining heads and pipes of the sprinkler system. Boone was dead wrong. He had to be, and she would prove that to him. Her stomach churned nastily and she dashed outside into the field behind the stables where she lost her dinner.

After getting sick, she felt clammy and lightheaded. Erin went back into the stables where she sat on a hay bale while her stomach settled. She had been queasy several times lately and she wondered if she was coming down with something.

Once she was feeling better and more in control of her emotions, she examined each structure thoroughly and then stood outside to view them. Her opinions were only more deeply confirmed. The structures were sound. The sprinkler systems were in place and the view was picturesque. She strode back to her house, slamming the door and kicking off her shoes, muttering about the man coming in and wanting to take charge and change the place when he knew nothing about it.

Boone stayed in the shadows outside before heading back to his house. He had seen her getting sick and he felt dreadful for upsetting her so much. At the same time, he was absolutely certain he was right about the stables. When the Stallion Pass fire chief and Perry agreed with him, their opinions added to Boone's worries.

He went through the house to the downstairs family room and plunked down beside the phone to pick it up and call Erin.

Erin's phone rang and she went to pick it up, but when she looked at the caller ID and saw it was Boone calling she removed her hand. He would think she was still at the stables, and she didn't want to argue with him any further tonight.

The following night on their dinner date, she was cool, but he poured on the charm, and before the evening was over, she forgot the stables completely. In spite of being angry with him, she missed him and wanted his arms around her.

He was already gone when she got up the next day.

The second day he was gone, she was eating breakfast as Hettie bustled around the kitchen. Erin grew warm and could hardly focus on what Hettie was saying as her stomach became queasy.

"Do you want this roast frozen?" Hettie asked.

Erin got up to run from the room, just making it to the bathroom in time to lose her breakfast.

She got a cold cloth to wipe her face and turned to see Hettie in the doorway.

"Are you all right, Erin?"

"I don't know what's wrong. I can't keep breakfast down anymore."

Hettie's eyes narrowed. "Erin, you better see Dr. Grayson."

"I'll be all right."

Hettie's lips firmed and her gaze ran over Erin's figure. "You should see the doctor."

Erin nodded, but when Hettie had looked speculative, she knew what Hettie was thinking. Erin felt weak in the knees and this time it was from the realization that she might be pregnant!

Eight

First she tried a home pregnancy test and then she went to her doctor in Stallion Pass. After a thorough exam and tests, once she was again dressed in her navy skirt and blouse, Erin sat in shock as the news was confirmed by Thomas Grayson, M.D., family doctor for her all her life.

"Dr. Grayson, I can't be. It's just not possible," she said, remembering that Boone had used protection.

"It's not impossible," he said, and explained the percentages for birth control measures to fail.

Stunned, she barely heard him and left his office with her head spinning. She had a prescription for prenatal vitamins and the name of an obstetrician in San Antonio.

She sat in her car staring into space, remembering all of Boone's remarks that he would never marry. The last thing on earth she wanted was for him to feel trapped into marriage. But raising a child on her own?

If he had spent all his growing-up years shouldering responsibility for being the man of the family and helping his mother and siblings, Erin knew that he would not be the kind of man to walk out when he learned that she was carrying his child.

But there was no way she wanted him to marry her out of a sense of duty.

Erin burst into tears, giving vent for about two minutes to crying and then raising her head. Tears wouldn't help and her depression wouldn't do anything for the baby, no matter how tiny. Instead, she needed to think.

She was financially well fixed and able to support a baby. Every man who worked on the Double T Ranch would be wonderful to her child and Uncle Perry would be like a grandfather, so there were plenty of father figures.

She raised her head, beginning to make plans and knowing she had to get Boone out of her life immediately. That thought cut like a knife, and she gripped the steering wheel until her knuckles were white. She looked down the tree-lined street with shops along a strip surrounding the doctor's office and knew she would remember this moment the rest of her life.

"I love you, Boone," she whispered, knowing she did, and that this child had been conceived in love. And she would love his baby. For the first time a thrill went through her and she smiled. She was going to be a mother. A baby! Boone's baby! Joy replaced all the fears, uncertainties and shock that had just tormented her. Her own baby. Hers and Boone's. She did love him, but there was no way she wanted him tied to her when he didn't love her or want to be married to her.

Their baby! She smiled and held her flat tummy and closed her eyes.

She would be busy and she could get along without Boone and that separation was going to happen anyway. He had made that clear from the first, so now it would just be sooner instead of later.

Part of Boone would always be hers. He was the love of her life whether he loved in return or not and she was going to cherish this precious baby of his.

She sobered. If she could get Boone to give up the ranch and move away, he wouldn't even know about the baby until there was time and distance between them and he had forgotten her and moved on.

With his business moving to Stallion Pass, though, he was going to find out. She just wanted to get him out of her life before then. She wouldn't be able to get him out of her heart as easily, but if she broke it off with him he would be less likely to come charging in feeling obliged to marry her and give the baby a name.

If she stopped seeing him, he would move away and find someone else and soon forget her. The realization hurt, but Erin knew it was the only way to let Boone be the free spirit he wanted to be. She loved him too much to tie him down as a reluctant husband.

She put the key in the ignition and started the engine, but then paused and reached for her cell phone. One of the most important things she had to do was to break tonight's date with Boone. She couldn't talk to him until she had her thoughts organized.

First, she contacted her best friend in Stallion Pass, Tina Courtland, and asked her if she could come stay the night. To her relief, Tina was happy to invite her friend over.

Instead of driving home to the ranch, Erin went straight to the gated area where Tina lived, driving along winding, tree-lined streets to an elegant Georgian redbrick home. She let herself in with a hidden spare key and sat down in the kitchen to call Boone and break their date.

Sunlight streamed through the kitchen windows and Erin could hear the ticking of the tall clock in the hall while she listened to the ringing of Boone's phone.

He was still out on the ranch, so it was a simple matter to leave a message for him. "Boone," she said, trying to inject cheerfulness in her voice, "I had to go to town today and I talked to an old friend. I'm staying with her tonight to catch up on her latest news. I'll be at Tina Courtland's. I'll see you tomorrow. Sorry to break our dinner date, but Tina and I haven't seen each other for over a month. If you need to get in touch, I have my cell phone."

Erin replaced the receiver, took her cell phone from her purse and switched it off.

After five, Erin heard her tall, brunette friend come in the back door. An attorney, Tina shared an office with ten other lawyers. Her hazel eyes were filled with curiosity when she saw Erin.

"Hi. I'm glad you're here!" she said as she shed her suit jacket and kicked off her pumps. "I don't have to work on a case or a brief or do any research. Let's have a cold drink and you tell me what brings you to my house—you sounded out of sorts on the phone."

"It's a long story," Erin said, watching Tina drop her purse and get out glasses. "Tea? Wine? Pop?"

"Just ice water, please. Thanks for putting me up."

"Sure. Anytime, Erin. I've missed catching up with you for way too long now." Tina studied Erin and then turned to get ice.

"I've been hearing all sorts of rumors about you and a Colonel Boone Devlin who inherited the Double T. Does this visit involve this colonel?" Tina demanded.

"Yes, it does. Let's get those cold drinks because it's a long story."

Sitting in comfortable chintz-covered chairs, Erin told Tina about everything, including the doctor's visit today.

"You're pregnant! How wonderful!" Tina got up and hugged Erin. "So marry the guy. It seems pretty simple."

"No, it's not. He's not into marrying at all, I told you that."

Tina waved her hand and went back to her seat to sip a glass of white wine as she smiled at Erin. "He'll change his mind."

"I don't want to trap him into marriage. He'll feel duty-bound to ask me, but that isn't what I want."

"Don't be so hasty," Tina advised. "He sounds like a man who knows how to make up his own mind. You won't be trapping him. That's ridiculous. Do you love him?"

"Yes, I do," Erin said quietly, hurting and knowing that Tina wasn't getting the full picture, but then Tina had never heard Boone talk about his aversion to marriage and his feelings on the subject.

"You can stay here as long as you like, but you know you have to go home sometime."

"I know. I just want to get a little space between us. He's not the patient type. Maybe he'll get tired of being put off."

"He's the father. You'll *have* to tell him about the baby."

"I know that. When he learns the truth, I'll have a battle on my hands. I just need time."

"Well, tell me more about this Boone Devlin. I never thought I'd see the day that *you'd* be all starry-eyed. He may surprise you about getting married, you know. Men have changed their stand on marriage before."

"Not this man." Erin went on to explain Boone's background.

The two friends talked for hours until Tina yawned hugely and announced, "I have to call it a night and you should, too. You can stay as long as you'd like as far as I'm concerned, but think about what I said."

"I'm going home tomorrow. I just wanted to get my thoughts straight before I see him again. Thanks, Tina."

"Anytime. He sounds like a good guy. He may be just as in love as you are."

"I know he's not," Erin said. "He couldn't be in love with *me*.'

"I'm betting on a wedding."

"Then you lose," Erin said as her friend shook her head and headed out of the room. Erin went to the guest bedroom that she had stayed in many times before, looking at the familiar king-size bed covered in a red, white and green quilt.

Erin slept soundly, despite her worries. The next morning she drove home to the ranch. Boone's car was in his garage and the pickup was gone, so she knew he was out on the ranch. It was just a matter of time.

He called half an hour after she arrived home, and they made a dinner date for the evening. She had to face him and break off relations and the sooner the better.

That evening she bathed and dressed in a red blouse and jeans, studying her figure. Her stomach was as flat as ever and she looked slender and unchanged from the way she had looked a month ago.

She brushed her hair and finally slipped on loafers and went downstairs to wait for Boone.

When he rang the doorbell, her hands were clammy and butterflies caused tremors to her insides. As she opened the door, her heart thudded. More tanned than ever from his days at the ranch, Boone looked full of energy, sexy and as handsome as ever. She glimpsed his gray shirt and jeans before he swept her up in his arms and kissed her.

Inhaling his aftershave, relishing the strength of his arms around her, she closed her eyes. All the time she kissed him in return, she wondered if it might be the last kiss between them. She ran her hands along his muscled arms, up across his strong shoulders. With reluctance, she pushed away.

He frowned. "I've missed you," he said, studying her intently and leaning down to kiss her again.

She slipped away out of his arms. "Come in. We need to talk."

She could hear him behind her as she walked to the kitchen. "Would you like a drink?"

"Sure. I'll have a beer." He pulled out a chair and watched her move around the room. She fixed a glass of ice water for herself and a beer for him and then sat down facing him.

"This looks serious," he said, his eyes narrowing. She gazed at the thick fringe of black lashes that made his eyes so sexy. If only— She stopped her thoughts right there.

"It is serious," she said. "I've had time to think and I don't like where our relationship is going. I want marriage, Boone, or I want out," she said, her heart thudding because she guessed this would be the one ultimatum that would send him on his way.

He stared at her and tilted his head, taking a long drink of beer but watching her all the time. She made an effort to gaze steadfastly back at him and not fidget.

"That's a change of heart on your part because you told me before that you didn't have to have marriage," he said finally.

"I've thought it over and I do," she said, beginning to feel more fluttery because she wasn't getting the reaction she expected so far. Yet she guessed the whole conversation was going to end within another few minutes.

"I've told you from the first my feelings about marriage," he said quietly.

She nodded. "I know you have and I know what I want, so if we can't agree, then we need to break things off."

"That's what you really want?" he asked, reaching across the table to caress her cheek.

Her heart pounded, and she wanted to cry out that no, that wasn't what she wanted at all. She wanted him with all her heart, but she *did* want marriage. She wasn't that far from the truth about the relationship. But she wanted marriage with a man who loved her. Who would stay with her. She didn't want to tell him goodbye, but there was no choice.

"That's what I want," she said firmly.

He continued to stare at her and she stared back, feeling the tension between them increase. Finally he stood up. "I suppose there's only one thing for me to do then and that's get out of your life."

Nodding, she stood. "If you can't commit to marriage, then that's the way it has to be," she said, certain of his reaction now.

"I'll think about it, Erin, but I just can't see settling down again to what I did for most of my life. I still want a break from it. Maybe ten years from now I'll change my mind, but not yet."

"While I, on the other hand, want a husband."

He inhaled deeply, frowning slightly. "It was wonderful, darlin'."

"It was. But I'd say that we're through," she said, her heart a drumroll while she tried to ignore the hurt that increased each second.

"If that's what you want, then I suppose so. I need you, want to be with you, but marriage—I'm not ready."

"I didn't think you were."

They walked to the front door. "I'm just trying to face the future, Boone."

He ran his finger along her cheek lightly and then caressed her throat. "You're special, darlin'. I'll think about it." He brushed a kiss on her cheek and then he was gone. She closed the door and leaned against it and let tears spill down her cheeks. He was gone and that was the only way, the only answer. She didn't want him to feel trapped or to offer to marry her out of guilt. And he would when he found out about the pregnancy, but by that time they would each have other lives.

She brushed away the tears, squared her shoulders and began to plan for a future without him. She needed a nursery and she also realized there was the possibility of just packing and going away for the last few months. Women had done that for aeons and then returned with a baby. She could afford to go away, and she had close friends scattered across Texas and other states and two close friends in London where she could stay.

She sat down on the foot of the stairs and put her head in her hands to give vent to tears again. She loved Boone and she already missed him and she wanted him in her life.

She had guessed his reaction correctly though, because he hadn't argued or offered other suggestions or even tried to talk her into staying together. He had made his feelings clear. She wondered if she would ever stop missing him. If her heart would ever stop hurting.

Through the warm summer night Boone walked in stony silence back to his mansion. He hurt more than he had ever guessed it was possible to hurt. He was angry with Erin, feeling as if she had done an about-face, changing abruptly on the subject of marriage from what she had told him before. The past two days he had missed her incredibly and had been counting the minutes until they could be together again. And then to get an ultimatum to marry or get out—he was still in shock.

It wasn't even eight o'clock yet. Without noticing what he was doing, he went through his gate, let himself into the house and tossed the key onto a table. Then he walked out onto the patio.

Her ultimatum was unlike her. She hadn't looked happy, either, but the woman knew what she wanted. He was hurt and he didn't like what had happened—hadn't they had a good thing between them? He kicked a rock with the toe of his new western boots that he had bought to impress Erin. Show her he could fit in on this ranch. This confrontation had come out of the blue. And he was astonished how much he had been looking forward to being with her tonight. He had thought she would feel the same.

"Serves you right," he said to himself, thinking of women who had shed tears over him when they had parted and how blithely he had kissed them goodbye and figured they would recover soon.

He wondered whether *he* would ever recover. The notion shook him. Of course he would. He could always come back and offer to marry her. If he didn't wait too long and some local guy caught her fancy.

Marriage—he remembered diapers and runny noses and bills and lost sleep and fights. It wouldn't have to be like that now because the bills could be paid easily and nannies could be hired. But he didn't want to be rooted to this ranch the rest of his life, tied here just as Erin was and wanted to be.

No, no marriage for him. He was going to miss her. Hell, maybe he even loved her some, but they hadn't known each other long and soon she should fade from his memory.

He swore softly and kicked another rock. Unhappiness and anger filled him and he was tempted to go right back and try to argue her out of this decision, but he knew that was useless. He remembered that night in the parking lot.

When Erin made up her mind, it was set. It had been grand and she was sexy and wonderful, but he would have to get along without her. Boone sighed. No matter how he argued with himself he was in for another sleepless night. He turned to look at the mansion he had inherited and knew he didn't want to spend another night in it alone.

He didn't even want to stay on the ranch tonight. All he

could think about was Erin. Disappointment filled him. Was *this* the reason she had stayed in town last night? How long had she been thinking these things over? He wished she had discussed her feelings more with him, yet he knew there really wasn't anything to discuss. She wanted marriage and he didn't. End of discussion.

He went back into the house, gathered his things and left, locking up and getting one of the men to drive him to the airport so he could fly home to Kansas. Maybe he could get his mind off Erin.

The next day Erin learned from talking to Perry that Boone was no longer on the ranch and she wondered if he had gone for good. She would not have been surprised.

She began to plan in earnest for a nursery and to consider what she would do the last months of her pregnancy.

It was Monday of the next week as she wrote a business letter when she heard the doorbell ring.

Curious who would be at the door, Erin hurried to answer it, opening the door to find Boone standing on her porch. She stared at him in surprise, trying to ignore the leap in her heartbeat.

"May I come in?" he asked.

Trying to ignore her racing pulse, she stepped back. "Of course."

"I'd like to talk to you."

"Sure, Boone. Come in," she said, stepping back to let him enter. She caught a whiff of his aftershave that stirred memories that she couldn't afford to think about now.

"Are you eating breakfast?" he asked as his boot heels scraped the polished floor.

"No, I wasn't," she answered quickly.

Boone's gaze traveled over her and she was tempted to

smooth her hair. Suddenly she was aware of her T-shirt and cutoffs, the butterfly clip in her hair that let tendrils escape and curl around her face.

Feeling self-conscious with him following her, she led him into the family room and motioned for him to sit down. "Would you like coffee?" she asked.

"Sure," he said. As soon as she headed toward the kitchen, he stood and followed.

Erin heard him coming behind her and she tried to ignore him as she moved around the kitchen, getting out the coffeepot and filling it with water. Her stomach was queasy this morning and now she wished she hadn't offered Boone coffee because sometimes the slightest smells sent her over the edge.

Grimly, she worked until he took the pot out of her hands. When his fingers brushed hers so lightly, her heart missed beats and her breath caught.

"Go sit down. I can do this," he said.

She stared at him, and wondered what had caused him to take the coffeepot from her hands. He had never tried to keep her from doing anything before.

"Uncle Perry said that you'd left the ranch," she said.

"Yep. I flew back to Kansas City."

In minutes she sat across from him at the table while the brewing coffee filled the room with an aroma that made her stomach roll, and she began to find it difficult to concentrate on Boone or anything he was saying to her.

"I've hired a new pilot and I needed to stay and work with him," he said.

Tight-lipped, she nodded.

While he rambled on about his plans for his business, Boone studied her, sensing come kind of undercurrent that he couldn't identify and feeling something was awry.

Had she missed him as badly as he had missed her? When she had opened the door, she had looked fantastic, but now he was beginning to wonder if she was coming down with something or furious with him or hurt beyond measure. She was pale, which she hadn't been only a few minutes ago. Her fingers were locked together and her knuckles were white and her lips had firmed. The more he looked at her the more he decided that she must be enraged at him or devastated by the breakup.

"Erin, I've missed you," he said flatly, hurting and wanting to take her into his arms and bring back the sparkle in her eyes and her laughter.

She merely nodded and clamped her lips together more firmly.

"I like the ranch," he said, "but the house is big and empty and I need to get a little distance and rethink things."

She merely nodded, and his feeling that something was wrong grew.

"You don't have anything to say about it?" he asked.

She shook her head and grew a little pale.

"Do you feel well?" he asked, trying to guess what was wrong.

Her lips clamped together more. "No, I don't. Excuse me, Boone," she said and fled from the room.

He stared after her. She clearly was sick. He got up and trailed after her, wondering where she had gone, and then saw the closed bathroom door in the back hallway.

He walked to the door and waited.

"Erin, can I help?" he asked, concerned now because she was sick, which she should have just told him when she answered the door.

"No!"

He stared at the door and turned to go back to the kitchen

and pour his coffee. If she had lost her breakfast, he wondered if she would like some soda crackers and pop to calm her stomach. Maybe she had a twenty-four-hour virus, but he hadn't heard of one going around.

He went to the pantry to find crackers and got a bottle of pop, snapping it open and pouring a small glass. He put some crackers on a plate.

He sat back down to wait, and as time grew longer, he wondered if she had fainted. He stood to go see about her, when she came back through the door. She looked pale and distraught and he had to fight the urge to get up and take her in his arms and hold her.

"I got some crackers and pop for you if you want. That might settle your stomach."

"I'm fine," she replied firmly.

"You're not fine," he said. "Let's move over by the sofa and you lie down. I'll bring the crackers and pop."

"Boone, I'm fine," she said. "But we'll move." She hurried to the sofa and sat down, leaning back and closing her eyes as she rubbed her forehead.

"I'll stay with you today. Hettie is cooking at my house, so if there's anything you want, I can send her over here—"

"No, there isn't," Erin said, opening her eyes and looking alarmed. "And I'd rather be alone. Then I can sleep. How soon are you moving out?"

"Right away. I wanted to tell you before I told Perry, although I imagine he'll be glad to see me go."

"Uncle Perry doesn't dislike you."

"I feel like a real greenhorn around him."

She waved her hand and gazed at him. Boone wanted to hold her badly. He hurt and he wanted her to protest and ask him to stay at the ranch, but she was doing none of that. He couldn't resist. He grasped her hand, feeling how soft and warm she was. He moved close beside her on the sofa and felt her forehead.

"At least you don't have a temperature."

"No, I don't. I'm fine, really," she said, but he noticed she hadn't pulled her hand away. He rubbed her wrist lightly and wondered if her pulse had speeded as his own had when he touched her.

"I've really missed you, Erin," he said solemnly and watched her inhale deeply. Her lips firmed again and she sat up straighter.

"I've missed you, too, Boone, but I think our decision is for the best."

He studied her intently. She was telling him goodbye, giving him the cold shoulder, insisting she wanted him to move away. Yet why did he have the feeling that wasn't what she really wanted at all?

Was his own ego blinding him? He suspected that might be the case. The lady said go, so he should get out of her life.

"Bye, darlin'," he said softly, brushing her lips so lightly while his insides clenched and heated and he wanted her as he had never wanted a woman before.

"I'll let myself out, Erin. Don't move. I'll go out the back door so the front will still be locked. I'll stay with you today if you want or get you anything you need."

"I'm fine and I don't need you to get a thing. If you'll let yourself out, that's good," she said, putting her head back against the sofa and closing her eyes, and he knew he had been dismissed.

Hurting, he stood and gazed down at her, fighting the constant and increasing urge to bend down and take her in his arms. He wanted desperately to hold her. He turned abruptly and crossed the room, moving through the house without thinking while pain overwhelmed him. He wanted her badly. At the door he looked back and she hadn't moved.

"Erin—"

"I'm fine, Boone. I just want to be alone," she said, her voice sounding more firm than it had only a few minutes ago.

He left, closing the door quietly behind him and standing beside it. Something was wrong and he didn't know if it was just his own world that had crumbled and made him feel that way about everything else, or if something was really amiss that he wasn't getting. He went back inside quietly, starting to call to her, when he saw her go striding past the open hall door.

Startled, he stopped and then let himself out silently. He walked home slowly. She hadn't been in the bathroom sick to her stomach in pretense. He was certain of that because she had been pale as snow. But she didn't have a fever and she had looked fine just now. Not like someone up off a sickbed and creeping around the house.

Puzzled, he went home, thinking about her, forgetting that he intended to move today until he stepped inside the mansion and saw his packed boxes. He went through the house to the kitchen.

"Hettie," he said as he entered the kitchen. "I don't think Erin is well. She was sick to her stomach this morning."

Hettie busied herself at the sink without looking at him. "I wouldn't know."

"You cooked at her place yesterday. Was she feeling all right then?"

"Yes, sir," she said, banging pots and still keeping her back turned to him.

She obviously wanted him out of her kitchen. He suspected it was unanimous that everyone wanted him off the ranch. Perry knew things weren't right between Erin and him, but Boone thought that likely suited Perry just fine. The man probably figured Erin had seen the light and dumped him. Which it looks like she did, he thought glumly. She had probably dumped other guys in the past and Perry had been around to see this occur and had taken it all in stride.

She didn't exactly look as if she had a broken heart or was pining away without him.

He knew it was over between them and he needed to pack and go. He knew he couldn't stay at the Double T. He couldn't stand staying in that mansion by himself. It was too big and empty. It reminded him something was missing from his life.

He wasn't certain he could stay and watch Erin date some other guy. Possibly fall in love and get married. Just the thought tied him in knots.

Late in the afternoon, Boone drove back to the house to pack more of his belongings, but he moved slowly, his thoughts still wrapped up in Erin.

He didn't know he could want a woman as badly as he wanted her. Or hurt over one the way he hurt over her. A hurt that wasn't going away or diminishing. Instead, it was getting worse with each passing day.

He was tempted to call her and see how she was feeling. He tried to continue packing but gave it up. All he could think about was Erin, and he wondered what she was doing. Several times he reached for the phone only to put it down and tell himself that she would not want him to call.

He went over the morning again, remembering his strange conversation with Hettie who had been so cold and aloof with him.

When he stopped to think about it, Erin had been sick twice lately—when she ran out of the stable and this morning.

He stared into space and then a thought occurred to him as he remembered his mother fighting morning sickness with every pregnancy, and as a kid, he used to wonder why she kept having children.

"Oh, damn!" Boone stood up, his eyes round while shock hit him like a bolt of lightning. It couldn't be possible, could it? But then too many things fit—sickness that passed quickly, her abrupt breaking off the relationship.

Erin was pregnant with his child!

Stunned, he clutched his stomach, feeling sick himself, but then he reminded himself that he might be way off. He left his house, striding across the driveway to her door to punch the bell.

She swung open the door and she had none of the pallor of the morning. She looked great, even glowing, and he was reminded again with a gut punch how much he missed her.

"Can I come in and talk to you?" he asked.

"Yes," she said cautiously, stepping back.

He entered and heard her close the door behind him. Without waiting for her, he went to the family room and turned to face her.

"How're you feeling?"

"I feel fine now. I thought you were going to town."

"Did you feel fine yesterday morning?"

"Yes," she answered, looking puzzled, and he began to relax.

"I thought maybe you had morning sickness," he said evenly, holding his breath. "Erin, are you pregnant?"

Nine

Erin felt her heart plummet and her head spin. How had he guessed? And guessed so quickly? Surely just this morning hadn't given her away?

He steadied her, and she was aware of his fingers on her shoulder. She opened her eyes and stepped back so his hand fell away, but she was looking into his piercing blue eyes and she could feel that he could probably see the truth by just looking at her.

There was no use denying what he had said, because she couldn't hide the pregnancy forever.

"You're not obligated by this in any way, Boone. I made my own choices."

He paled, and she clutched her hand to her middle, hurting because it was obvious that her affirmation of his suspicions were not what he wanted to hear.

Boone turned away and raked his fingers through his hair and she gazed at his broad shoulders.

"Go home, Boone. This doesn't concern you anymore," she said stiffly, hurting more than ever. "I'm financially well fixed and can afford this baby and you don't have to be any part of this whatsoever."

He turned around to study her intently, and she was certain that he felt trapped and guilt was probably eating him up.

"I really mean it. Get out," she said. "Go. I'm fine. The doctor said the morning sickness will pass soon. I have a lot of support here."

"Hettie knows, doesn't she? But Perry doesn't."

"I haven't told Hettie, but she might have guessed. I haven't told anyone except my friend Tina."

"Erin, you were a *virgin*. That's my baby and there's only one answer. We need to do the right thing."

"Absolutely not. I know how you feel about marriage and I will not marry you."

He waved his hand in a dismissing motion. "That's easy to say now, but you won't want to say it later. Your baby needs a father."

"Boone, you of all people should know that kids can get along without a father. I have so many father figures on this ranch. Don't you know that Uncle Perry will be like a devoted grandfather to this baby?"

"I'm sure he will," Boone said between clenched teeth, "but that doesn't take away my responsibility—"

"Just stop right there," she said firmly. "I'm *not* marrying you. You can beg, cajole, plead, argue, but I will *not* do it. Let's get that straight this minute. I don't want to date you anymore. I want us to go our separate ways. Our relationship was a big mistake except that I have a sweet baby on the way and that's good."

"I don't believe you don't want to marry," he said in a gruff voice. His fists were still clenched, and he looked tense and wound tight.

"That's your problem, but I'm not changing what I'm telling you. I do not want you in my life again and I will not marry you," she said firmly and clearly and in a louder voice as if he couldn't get the facts straight. She could feel the tension between them escalating and a silent battle of wills was already under way.

"You're just saying and doing that to let me off the hook and to be nice."

"Boone, your ego is enormous. Can you get this? There is a woman here who is not all wrapped up in being with you. One does not turn down a marriage offer to 'be nice.' We're through. Finished. It's over!" she said loudly, leaning toward him as if he had suddenly become deaf.

"Last week you didn't feel that way at all," he said quietly.

"No, I didn't, but I've stepped back and taken a long look at the future and the present and I want you out of my life. I'm not marrying you because I'm pregnant. Not under any circumstances."

"I can't believe you."

"Am I the first woman to ever send you packing?"

"That's not it, dammit. You need me now and what we had was good," he argued, and she didn't want to listen or think about what he was saying. Trying to turn a deaf ear on his words, she glared at him.

"Dating was good for a time, but life changes. I know you've broken up with women many a time. You just changed how you felt about them. Remember?"

He stared at her, and her heart drummed while she faced him.

"You're sure?" he asked.

"I'm sure."

"Perry's going to kill me."

"No, he won't. But you might want to get off the ranch for a time."

"I'll tell him that I proposed to you and you turned me down."

"Don't say you weren't warned to stay out of his way," she said, barely knowing now what she was saying. She just wanted Boone to go because she was having difficulty trying to keep calm and in control of her emotions.

"Will you go to dinner with me tonight and discuss this?"

"No, I won't. We're through, Boone. This is goodbye, whether you live on the ranch or not."

He turned, striding out and slamming the door. She let out her breath and shook all over. He rang the bell and she started toward the door when he opened it. "Erin, I just can't walk away. Dammit, you have—"

"No, I don't have to do anything with you. Goodbye," she repeated, thankful she hadn't burst into tears the minute he had closed the door and wondering if he had come back to see if she had.

He slammed the door closed again, and she fought tears, finally giving vent to them. He wanted to marry her for all the wrong reasons. He wanted to date for the wrong reasons. There had been no joy from him about the confirmation of the news that she was pregnant.

She knew he felt trapped, just as she had thought he would. He had proposed out of duty and offered to stay with her out of duty.

Walking to the window, she watched him stride across the yard. If he had good sense, he would get off the ranch before Uncle Perry found out the truth. She could hide it briefly, but that was all. Especially if Hettie knew.

Erin went upstairs to her room and moved to the window where she could see out across the ranch. She put her head against the cool window. How easy it would have been to say yes, but all the joy would have gone out of their relationship.

She wanted a real home and a loving husband, not a marriage out of duty and obligation.

She cried quietly and then wiped her tears, telling herself to think about the baby and the joys the baby would bring. If only her parents had lived to see this baby. She wiped her eyes and moved away from the window, going to her father's room to move around, touching his things, looking at a family picture and looking at him and at her mother. She needed to call her sister and tell her, but Mary would be on the first plane to the ranch and she would tear into Boone if she saw him.

Erin smiled and looked out the window at the stables and corral and then her heart dropped. She saw Boone and her uncle talking. Several of the men gathered around them and as she watched, her uncle swung his fist and knocked Boone to the ground.

"Oh, no!" she cried out, turning to run, dashing down the stairs. Boone was a trained fighter, but she saw him take the blow without even trying to defend himself. She could just imagine what was happening and knew Boone might let her uncle and the others beat him senseless without lifting a hand against them.

"I told you to stay out of his way. You foolish, foolish man," she said without even realizing she was talking or what she was saying as she ran through the house and outside, racing across the lawn and the driveway.

Now more men circled Perry and Boone and she couldn't even see them. She could hear men yelling to Perry to hit him again and then others yelling at Boone.

Suddenly one of the cowboys blocked her path. It was Dusty Thatcher and he had his feet planted wide apart, his hands on his hips as he blocked her.

"Dusty, you get out of my way."

"Erin, you go on back home. This is between the men. Your

daddy would want me to send you home and that's exactly what I'm doing, and if I have to, I'll pick you up and carry you there."

"Dusty, I've been having a difficult time. Are you going to upset me when I'm pregnant?" she snapped. "My daddy wouldn't want any of you to make me lose this baby, now, would he? This will be his first grandchild."

The man's eyebrows shot up and his jaw dropped and he stared at her. "No, ma'am, they wouldn't. But you can't—"

"Oh, yes I can," she said, brushing past him.

Instantly, Dusty jumped in front of her and pushed between the men, talking to them. Cowboys she had known all her life turned to stare at her and she saw the surprise on each man's face as Dusty must have relayed her message. Suddenly they were quiet except for the blow as Perry's fist connected again on Boone's jaw and he sprawled back in the dirt.

She walked up and faced Perry.

"Dammit," he said, "who let you in here, Erin? You go home—"

"I'll tell you the same thing I told Dusty. Do you want to be upsetting me when you shouldn't? Do you really want to tangle with a pregnant woman?"

Perry blinked and lowered his fists. "Are you all right?"

She nodded. "I will be if you'll leave me alone and I can go home and not be so mightily upset."

"Erin, you know none of us want to upset or hurt you," Perry said, sounding instantly contrite.

Boone stood up, weaving, and then he straightened. She barely glanced at him as Perry shot Boone a deadly glance and then turned away. "C'mon, boys. Let's go." He looked over his shoulder. "Sorry, Erin," Perry said, giving her a narrow look.

They began to walk away and she glanced at Boone. "Let's go into the stable. There's a first-aid room."

"I'm not going to bleed to death. Let's head to your house before they change their minds," Boone said dryly, and she nodded.

He was bleeding badly and his eyes and mouth were puffed up. His shirt was torn and hung in shreds on him. He limped, but she let him hobble along beside her on his own.

"You could have defended yourself," she said, angry with all of them.

"He was right. I would have done the same thing if the situation had been reversed."

"Please! The sooner you are off this ranch, the better it will be. 'Course, it's your place, so if you want to stay where you're not wanted, there's nothing any of us can do about it, but don't expect much cooperation from the men."

"I wouldn't expect a shred of cooperation from them and you're not in any danger of losing the baby over watching me getting beaten to a pulp. That malarkey isn't working on me. Remember, I've been going through pregnancies since I was a kid. I'm an old hand at it and almost had to deliver Gregg myself. And I had to drive my mom to the hospital."

"You were eleven years old!"

"That's right. I sat on the phone book and encyclopedias," he mumbled. "It hurts to talk. Tell you 'bout it later."

"I don't care to hear about it," she said stiffly. At the back gate she paused. "I think I should drive you to the emergency room in Stallion Pass."

"No way. Don't argue, either."

"You are one incredibly stubborn man. Come on." She led the way through the back entry to the first downstairs bathroom and Boone turned to her.

"I think I should just shower and then maybe you can tape me up."

She shut her mouth and left him, pulling the door closed

forcefully, but then she opened it instantly. He had started to pull off his shirt and was grimacing as he tried to raise his arms.

"Stop," she said. "I'll cut your shirt off. It's a rag now anyway."

She hurried to get scissors and came back to find him sitting on the edge of the tub. "If you can get to the bathroom off the front bedroom downstairs, it's big and more comfortable."

When he nodded, she moved out of his way. As he hobbled beside her in the hall, she looked at him. "Want me to help support you?"

"Nope. I think I might have bruised ribs."

"Boone, let's go to the hospital."

"I'll be all right. I've had worse injuries before."

In the large bathroom he showered and then emerged with a towel around his middle. Her breath caught when he opened the door and squinted at her through puffed, blackened eyes.

"Boone! You look terrible!" she exclaimed, horrified by the sight of him and afraid how badly he was hurt. "Let me take you to a doctor."

"It just looks worse than it is. Give me some stuff to put on these cuts and some bandages for the biggest ones. The rest are bruises and they'll heal."

"You can't see."

"Yes, I can. Got any ice packs?"

"Yes," she said, hurrying to get gauze and bandages and antiseptic ointment and trying to ignore her racing pulse at the sight of him in a towel. His face was mauled and he had cuts and bruises, but he still had a magnificent, strong male body that she was intently aware of.

"Sit down," she said, and bustled around him, trying to ignore firm muscles and bare body and get his cuts tended. Finally she stepped away. "I'll get ice packs and go to your house and bring you some clothes."

She suspected she should just send him home and ignore him, but she also felt guilty for what had happened to him. She hurried out, going to his house and switching off the alarm, hurrying to find him fresh clothes. She saw the packed bags and wondered now when he would move.

Shaking her head, she gathered clean briefs, jeans and a T-shirt. "There, Boone Devlin. Get dressed and get out of my hair," she mumbled as she hurried back to her house, guessing that he would stay through dinner.

She found him lounging on the sofa in the family room. He sat up carefully when she entered the room. When she handed him the clothes, he looked up at her through slits from his swollen eyes.

"Going to help me get into these?" he asked.

"I don't know whether you're teasing or not, but no, I'm not. If you can't get your briefs on by yourself, then I'm calling an ambulance and they'll help you and take you to the hospital where you belong!"

She thought she saw his swollen lips purse slightly and then he groaned. She left him to get dinner on, wondering if she would have him not only for dinner but for the night.

She cooked soup, which he sipped carefully, and then he wanted a beer. He had dressed in the jeans but nothing else. She didn't know if he was wearing the briefs or if they were folded up beneath the T-shirt and socks, but she didn't care.

"I suppose a beer is all right since you're not on any medication," she said, going to get the drink and pouring it into a glass for him since she didn't think there was any way possible he could drink from a bottle.

"Talk about stubborn," she said, knowing he should go to the hospital.

"What?"

"You should let me take you to a doctor and you know it. How will you sleep tonight?"

"Don't know, but I'm not going to the hospital. Don't suppose you'd let me stay here in case I need something?" he asked mournfully.

"Of course," she said, rolling her eyes. "Stay tonight and I'll see who can stay with you tomorrow night."

He nodded. "It hurts to talk, Erin."

"Then stop talking to me," she said in exasperation.

"You keep talking to me. I can't hug you, but it would be nice if you'd just sit with me. It takes my mind off the pain."

"I will, but let me get some ice packs." In minutes she perched on the end of the sofa while he lay back against pillows at the other end and had ice packs all over his head and body.

"I am so put out with Uncle Perry—"

"Don't be," Boone urged. "You could at least marry me to give our child a name and then you could get divorced if you don't want to be married."

"If you keep talking about that, I'm leaving," she threatened. "As a matter of fact, I doubt if you should talk at all."

"All right, I'll stop," he agreed. "What would it take to get you to give my back a light massage? It would really help my aches."

When she nodded, he removed the ice packs, sat up straighter and turned around. She sat close behind him, massaging his back and being careful of the cuts and bruises, rubbing his shoulders and neck, avoiding his ribs.

"You won't fire any of them, will you? I'd feel terrible if you did."

"No. I won't fire anybody."

Her hands paused and then Erin continued massaging his rock-hard muscles, knowing he could have flattened Perry so easily. Had he done so, he would have had to fight all the rest of the men, but he probably would not have been hurt as badly.

"Uncle Perry will be happy for me when he calms down. Once this baby arrives, he'll be just delighted to be a real grandfather. His boys are grown, but neither one has married and he longs for grandchildren. He's told me that." She stood up. "I'm tired and I'm going to bed. I'll get you anything you want, but you're on your own. You can sleep in that downstairs bedroom."

He nodded. "I'm fine, Erin. Thanks for rescuing me."

She left him, feeling guilty and knowing she was deserting him to a night of pain, but she wanted to break things off and start getting over him, and having him under her roof was not helping. Having given him a massage hadn't helped, either.

Boone lay back, groaning, knowing she was right. He should have gone to the hospital. He probably should have defended himself, but he couldn't see hitting Perry and he didn't blame the man for his anger.

He turned his thoughts to Erin. She had to let him marry her. Did she really want him out of her life so badly? Or was this just because she knew how he felt about marriage?

He suspected the latter. He drew a breath, groaned when it hurt, and thought about their future. Would he be trapped if he married her? His first reaction had been a feeling of entrapment, but would he really feel that way?

The past few days without her in his life had been miserable.

He thought about the days since he had met Erin. And the nights. The magical nights when she could set his blood boiling and demolish him with her kisses. Just thinking about her made him want her in his arms and the thought of moving away from the ranch was repugnant.

He didn't want her out of his life. She was the most wonderful, awesome, interesting woman he had ever known. She was a mystery, intelligent, capable, unpredictable, sexy. Would it be a trap to be married to her? What was even a bigger question, was he already in love with her?

A baby on the way and diapers and all he had dreamed about getting away from for years.

But this was different. It was Erin, not a parent and siblings. Erin and his own baby. His pulse jumped at the thought, and he knew he'd better think long and hard about the future before he messed it up for good.

He got up and walked to a mirror, wondering if Perry had broken his nose. It hurt as if it was broken, and he supposed tomorrow he should go see a doctor. If Mike or Jonah heard about the fight, both of them would split their sides that he had taken such a beating, but if they found out why, he suspected that they would want to pound him themselves for getting Erin pregnant.

He limped to the bedroom she had told him he could have and eased down on the bed. Every bone in his body hurt, and he knew he was going to hurt even more in the morning. He tried to get comfortable and thought about Erin, upstairs, asleep alone in her bed, a baby started now. His baby.

He drew a deep breath, bit it off abruptly as pain shot through him. He wanted Erin. And their baby. *Their baby.*

Was this love? He didn't want to think about life without Erin, and now he didn't want to leave the ranch and leave Erin and his baby.

The next morning he slipped out of her house before dawn, hoping he would not encounter Perry or any other cowboy who worked at the Double T. He went through his house, fixed his own breakfast and hurt all over. It was an eternity before he could call Mike and ask the name of a doctor. By noon he had seen a doctor, had X rays taken, his ribs announced as badly bruised, and his cuts tended. To his relief, his nose was not broken and he could see a little better today as the swelling was starting to go down.

He got a hotel room and spent the night in Stallion Pass, lounging around the hotel and trying to recuperate and sort out his feelings about Erin. Whatever they were, he knew one thing—he missed her dreadfully.

He did not want to break off relations, stop dating, go separate ways, and he was certain she was doing this because she didn't want him to feel trapped into marriage.

He didn't want to face the future without her. Did he love her? Boone asked himself the question. Never before had he felt about a woman the way he did about Erin. No denying that one. Never before had he wanted one to the extent he wanted Erin. Particularly after making love as much as they had.

"I love you, Erin," he whispered in the empty hotel suite. "I do love you," he whispered again and he knew it was true. He was in love and she couldn't possibly mean that she wanted him out of her life. Not now. Not after learning that a baby was on the way.

He was in love. The realization staggered him because he had never expected it to happen.

She had to let him into her life. It was his baby, too. Yet he was nervous and uncertain. If she said she wanted him out of her life, that might be exactly what she had meant.

Her declaration that she wanted him to go might have been an ultimatum that she intended him to follow. If so, there would be nothing he could do to change her mind. On the other hand, if she was in love with him, then he didn't want to give up and pack and go.

He was in love. The idea was so novel he had to mull it over. He had never once been truly, deeply in love where he would possibly think about marriage or any kind of lasting relationship.

He needed to court Erin. He had rushed her into his bed, but she wasn't going to let him rush her into marriage, if he could get her into it at all.

The idea of life ahead without her was too empty to contemplate. He wanted her always. He loved her and he felt excited just thinking about Erin and marriage. He needed to get to a jeweler's. He needed to get well first and then start charting what he would do.

He had to get Erin to agree to let him stick around, to get her to go out with him again. He took a deep breath and grimaced when pain shot across his ribs.

Tomorrow he would begin.

"I'm in love," he whispered, stretching out on his bed and closing his eyes. He supposed he was. One thing he knew for an absolute certainty—he missed Erin like hell.

Two nights later the doorbell rang, and Erin went to the door. A glance out the window revealed that it was Boone on the porch. She was hardly at her best, dressed in a T-shirt and jeans, her hair in a casual ponytail. Shrugging, she opened the door to face him.

Her heart skipped a beat, and she took a deep breath. "This is a surprise. I thought maybe you had moved to town for good."

"Nope, I didn't."

"You look better," she said cautiously, thinking that he looked marvelous. He still had smudges around his eyes, but all the swelling was gone and the cuts were beginning to mend and there were fewer bandages.

"I saw a doctor."

"I'm glad. How about your ribs?"

"They're mending."

She shook her head. "I haven't seen Uncle Perry since that happened."

"I have, and I talked to him at length."

"And he didn't hit you again?" she asked, alarmed that Boone had already encountered her uncle.

"Nope. We got things sorted out between us."

"Well, good for you two," she said, shifting to another foot and wondering what he wanted.

"Can I come in and talk to you?"

"Boone, what's the point? I want to break things off and this isn't the way to do it. I want you to leave me alone."

"That's my baby, too, and I have a part in this. Suppose I were the one carrying the baby and trying to shove you out of my life?" he asked patiently.

"Well, first of all you have made it abundantly clear that you do not care about mommies or babies, having raised eight babies already. Second, you said you do not want to marry, except now, for all the wrong reasons. Boone, there's no more to be said. Case closed."

"Give me a chance, Erin. Talk to me."

"Is this about how you want to marry me now?"

"Might be, but I think I can put it a little more convincingly than that," he said solemnly.

"Forget it, Boone. Let's call it finished and done. Bye," she added softly and closed the door.

"It's about the stables," she heard through the door, so she opened it again.

"What about the stables?"

"Can I come in to talk?"

She took a deep breath and stepped back, watching him pass. He walked to the family room and sat on the sofa. "Come over here. I won't bite."

She sat on the end of the sofa.

"How are you feeling?" he asked.

"Still a little queasy in the mornings. Will you get to the point? What about the stables?"

"I don't want to worry you, but I've got brochures here," he said, pulling them out of his hip pocket and straightening them. "This is about new stables."

"We're not tearing down the old ones," she said in a firm voice.

"Look at these, Erin." He pointed to the pictures. "They're beautiful and have all sorts of advantages the old ones don't."

"This is your ranch, but according to the will, before you make changes, I have to approve them. I will never approve tearing down those stables without talking to the fire chief and Uncle Perry."

"Fine," Boone agreed. "You talk to each of them, but in the meantime, you can look at these brochures."

She took the brochures, aware of Boone moving closer, and then his hand was on her nape while he talked, caressing her lightly, and she wanted to close her eyes and let him wrap his arms around her, but she wasn't going to do that. "Boone, move your hand."

"You like me touching you. Tell me you don't."

"I don't now," she said softly, looking into his eyes. He was only inches away, and she wondered if he could hear her heart pounding.

"Give me room," she said breathlessly.

He placed his hand on her throat and gazed into her eyes. "Your pulse is racing."

"You know you do that to me, but that doesn't mean anything."

"What does it mean if I make your pulse race and make you sound breathless and you leave me wanting you and unable to sleep? What?"

"It means we haven't fully gotten over what we had, but we will."

"Is that so? What did we have?"

"Just some exciting times together. You said there was nothing to it, no future, no deep commitments—"

"I said too much and things I didn't mean."

"You meant every word of them." She stood. "Let's call it a night, Boone."

"Let me stay. It's lonesome and boring in that monster of a house without anyone there except me. Let's go get something to drink and just sit and talk."

She stared at him in consternation. He wasn't cooperating and she knew before long he would be his usual irresistible self and she would be in a deeper muddle than ever with him. Yet she was spending long, lonely evenings, too. She nodded. "All right, but it seems a step backward."

As they started down the hall, Boone moved closer and draped his arms across her shoulder.

She looked up at him briefly and then tried to ignore his embrace, but it was impossible because his fingers stroked her bare arm, an electrifying current following his touch.

As they moved around in the kitchen, the slightest accidental physical contact stirred more tingles in her.

"Let's sit out on the patio," he suggested, and she followed him to the door. He held the door for her and switched the lights off outside. Small yard lights and lights in the trees, as well as the pool lights, still gave enough illumination to clearly see each other. Boone pulled a chair close to hers.

"Erin," he said, setting down his beer and taking her hand. "Think about us. You know there's a world of difference between caring for siblings and caring for your own baby."

"I can't believe that you've had a complete turnaround. What I can believe is that guilt and honor will cause you to pursue marriage as if your life depended on my consent, but that isn't what I want," she explained patiently. "It really isn't."

He caressed her nape and then pulled her head closer, gazing into her eyes. "I don't want a future without you," he said, and her heart thudded so hard she was certain he would know it. He leaned the last bit of distance to kiss her, and his tongue entered her mouth, starting a storm of sensations and emotions. She kissed him in return and knew when he lifted her to his lap.

Finally she wrapped her arms around his neck and kissed him long and passionately before pushing against him and slipping off his lap to get back to her chair.

"You slow down. I don't believe you. You just want to do the right thing." She stood. "Boone, I'm getting tired."

He stood. "Let's go to dinner tomorrow night. I miss you and I want to straighten all this out."

"That translates to I want to get you to do things my way."

"Maybe, but I'm not so sure about your protests. I think you're saying no for the wrong reasons. If you didn't love me and really wanted me out of your life, I'd go, but I don't think that's it, just like you don't believe that I mean what I say."

"Boone, I saw your reaction when you realized I was pregnant. It was not joy and love."

"I was shocked. It wasn't something I expected. That doesn't mean I haven't had time to think things over and to change how I've always felt about babies and marriage."

"I don't think so," she said, taking his arm to lead him to the door, where she turned to face him.

"Go to dinner with me Saturday night, Erin."

"What's the point in dragging things out?"

"The point is, I want to be with you. Just go out to dinner with me. We've had a good time together and we'll have a good time Saturday night."

She sighed. "Going out together isn't going to change things."

"Doesn't have to change anything except me sitting around alone and missing you. All right, darlin'?"

"It seems so pointless."

"I want you to go with me," he said, placing his hands on her shoulders. He stroked her shoulders and then framed her face with his hands. Desire burned in his blue eyes and she wanted to let go and trust and believe him, but too well she remembered the look on his face when he had found out she was pregnant, and remembered all his declarations against marriage.

"Erin," he said, "I love you."

She closed her eyes, thinking how she had dreamed of hearing those words, longed for them, fantasized about them, but now she couldn't believe them. She shook her head and opened her eyes to gaze into his. "You don't really mean that."

"Yes, I do, darlin'," he said, pulling her into his arms to hold her close. He stroked her head. "You'll see. Just give me a chance."

She looked up at him and met his gaze and there was no mistaking the desire that blazed in depths of blue. She stood on tiptoe, pulling his head down to her to kiss him. As tongues touched, his arms tightened around her, holding her against him, and she felt his arousal. He leaned back against the door and cupped her bottom, pulling her closely to him while he kissed her. His hand caressed her back while he continued to hold her tightly with his other arm.

Her heart thudded, and longing swamped her, wanting everything with him and wanting to believe him, yet scared to let go and trust.

He slipped his hands beneath her shirt to cup her breasts, stroking her nipples, and she moaned softly, finally pushing against his chest.

"Slow down, Boone. I mean it."

He stroked her hair away from her face while she pulled her shirt in place. "I want you, Erin," he said.

"I'll see you tomorrow night," she said quietly, and opened the door. He gazed into her eyes and she clutched the door, knowing she needed to stay right where she was and not walk into his arms again.

He brushed a light kiss on her lips and turned away. "Tomorrow night about six," he called over his shoulder.

She nodded her head and closed the door, her heart pounding with joy that she tried to bank because she didn't really believe that he was truly in love. Not a love to last.

But oh, if he did— Her breath caught and she stopped following that line of thought. Instead, she remembered the moment he had learned that she was pregnant and how he had looked appalled and sounded distraught and unhappy.

Her smile faded while reality and grim facts took hold. Memories of his statements about marriage were as clear as if he had just said them to her. In three days she knew he couldn't have had a change of heart about something he had felt strongly about for years.

Her joy vanished, and she clutched her hands around her middle. There were some rocky times ahead. Tomorrow night she should tell him goodbye and stop this futile pursuit of his when he didn't really mean it.

She was not marrying the man when he was doing it out of a sense of duty.

She shivered and was swamped with longing and taunting memories that made her want to toss aside reason and hope that someday he would fall in love.

She knew she couldn't do that. Go out tomorrow night, break it off for good.

She went to bed and lay in the dark feeling lonely and forlorn and trying to concentrate on the baby until her thoughts brightened and she finally fell asleep.

As if conjured up by her gloomy feelings, the next day a rainstorm came up about noon. Black clouds gathered on the horizon, whipping up and spreading across the sky with surprising speed while lightning split the summer sky. They needed rain, so it should be welcome, but she didn't particularly want to go out to dinner tonight in the rain.

It would be more cozy to curl up in the house, but she didn't want to get cozy with Boone when she was going to have to tell him goodbye.

As she made calls and then got some ranch brochures ready to mail, the house darkened until she had to switch on lights. She moved through the dark house and looked at the surface of the swimming pool. The water rose and fell and the wind whipped up tiny waves.

Gusts tore at flowers, ripping loose petals and sending them tumbling through the air while the trees bent and shook. Lightning flashed and thunder boomed liked cannons. She went upstairs to look outside when a big clap of thunder rumbled, and then lightning flashed a blue-white brilliance and there was another ear-splitting bang.

Rain poured down in gray sheets, a deluge opening up while more lightning flashed. She wondered where Boone was and if he was out on the ranch somewhere and if he could get to cover.

She laughed at herself. The man had been in Special Forces. This was a rainstorm.

Feeling restless, she went back downstairs, and as she crossed the kitchen, she saw the first orange lick of flame.

She blinked, rushing to the window. An orange flame danced along the stable roof.

Ten

Chilled to the bone and terrified, wondering what horses were inside, she raced to the phone and yanked it up to call Perry and sound the alarm.

She called the emergency numbers and then tossed down the phone as she ran outside and sprinted through light rain to the burning stable.

As she ran, all she could think about were Boone's warnings about firetraps. Surely the sprinkler system would put out the fire in minutes.

Men were already there, getting out horses, and she raced inside. Some horses had gotten out into the run on their own, but others were in stalls that for one reason or another weren't open.

"Get out of here, Erin!" Perry yelled, but she dashed past him, yanking down a blanket to throw it over a horse's head and try to lead the frantic animal outside.

Even though the sprinklers had gone off, the fire raged out of control, hay going up instantly and the aged dry wood burning like tinder becoming a roaring fire that neither the sprin-klers nor the light rain could deter.

Leading a horse out into the run, she handed it over to a cowboy who then led it away from the stables. Horses whin-nied, and the rain still drizzled. Men yelled instructions as she ran back into the burning building.

Stunned, she drew back momentarily. The fire seemed to have doubled since she had led the last horse outside, but she could hear the frantic neighing and pawing of a horse still trapped.

"Boone was right," she said, without realizing she was talking to herself.

A timber cracked and she looked up as one of the large sup-porting beams that was consumed by fire broke loose and fell.

Flames shot high from the roof and could be seen all over the ranch. The dark plume of smoke had darkened and was spreading.

Far from the stable, Boone could see the fire.

He had been out on the ranch with Dusty, looking at new horses recently acquired when he had gotten a call from Perry. Terrified for Erin's safety, Boone raced for his pickup, while Dusty jumped in beside him. Boone floored the gas pedal, leaving the road and racing back toward the stables.

Cold fear gripped him because he knew if Erin learned about the fire, she would go out to save any horses caught in the burning stable.

Hunching over the steering wheel as the pickup bounced and raced across the ranch, Boone forgot Dusty beside him. He splashed through a creek, sending a spray of water high into the air and then raced out on the other side. He hit a rock and the pickup tilted, riding on two wheels a moment and then righting, dropping with a jolt that made it bounce when all four wheels hit the ground.

Boone heard Dusty swear, but he was barely aware of it. He could see the flames shooting high above the treetops then disappearing from sight as he raced down an incline.

When the stable came into view, while he was still hundreds of yards away, he saw Erin dash inside and his heart dropped.

The entire structure was a raging bonfire with flames shooting high, rain still coming down and men trying to move horses and fight the fire. The rain had slacked off to a fine mist, not enough to bring the fire under control, and a pumper truck was pouring water on the stable closest to the burning one.

Boone braked to a stop and flung out of the pickup, racing for the barn. Someone caught his shoulder and tried to stop him, but he shoved him away and ran inside. Someone else thrust a wet towel in his hand and he put it over his shoulder.

"Erin!"

She screamed as a beam fell, and Boone had to jump back. He ripped off his T-shirt and tied it around his nose and mouth, looking for her while his heart pounded wildly and fear gripped him.

Flames roared up the sides of the stable and above him. The entire place was an inferno and billows of smoke hid everything from sight.

"Erin!" he shouted. He felt as if his heart were being torn out.

He saw a shape in clouds of smoke, yards away, trying to lead a rearing, frightened horse.

Clinging to the halter, she was trying to get the frightened animal to come with her.

Boone leaped over the burning timber. "Go through the stall into the run! Get out, Erin," he yelled, yanking his T-shirt from his face and shoving it into her hands. "I'll get the horse."

He flung the towel over the horse's head and turned the horse to lead it out.

Covering her nose and mouth with his shirt, Erin moved ahead of him. While he watched her, Boone tried to keep the wild horse's eyes covered, battling to get it outside, but watching Erin who was a dark form lost in smoke and hidden by flames.

Heat licked at Boone and his lungs felt on fire. He couldn't see where he was going for a moment and then he saw the door looming and a slight figure go through it. Hurrying behind her, he led the horse out.

The instant he stepped outside, he released the halter. "Someone get this horse!" he shouted, and a man ran past him.

Boone scooped Erin into his arms. He strode away from the stable and then heard another loud crack and glanced over his shoulder to see what was left of the roof cave in with a crash that sent flames and sparks high into the air.

"The horses—" Erin gasped.

"They're out," he replied, not really knowing that, but wanting to calm her and knowing that if the last one wasn't out, there was no saving it now.

She tightened her arms around his neck. "You were right. The sprinklers did nothing to stop the fire."

"Don't worry about it, darlin'. Everyone's safe. We can rebuild. Shh. Are you all right?"

She raised her head and he gazed into her eyes that were brimming with tears. She wiped at them and he leaned forward to kiss her, a kiss that became long and fierce.

He strode away from the fire, leaving the others to deal with it and carrying Erin home. Her back door stood open where she had run outside when she'd first spotted the fire.

Boone strode through it, kicking the door shut and carrying her straight upstairs through her bedroom to her bathroom. She was shivering uncontrollably in his arms and he turned on the shower, stripping away her clothes and his and stepping into the shower with her. Warm water poured over her and gradually she stopped shivering.

"Boone, I was wrong—"

"Forget about it. The stable is gone. Doesn't matter now, darlin'. Ah, Erin, don't ever scare me like that again. You shouldn't have gone into that burning stable and risked yourself and our baby."

When she looked up at him, her eyes widened.

"Promise. Don't ever do anything like that again," he persisted. "I couldn't bear it if anything happened to you." He stood in the shower with water streaming over both of them and framed her face with his hands.

"Erin, I love you."

Erin thought she would faint with joy because there was no mistaking the need and sincerity in his voice this time.

When he kissed her, she wrapped her arms around him. In minutes he shut off the shower and grabbed a towel, drying her slowly, lightly running the towel over her. And then he picked her up to carry her to her bed where he made slow, tantalizing love to her.

Afterward, he held her tightly against him as they lay on their sides. "Darlin', this is the way it should be. So good, my love."

He trailed kisses over her and held her close and they lay locked in an embrace.

"I love you, have loved you for how long now and didn't even know how to recognize the real thing," he whispered. "Darlin', I'll never be able to say it enough—I love you."

She hugged him tightly. "I love you, Boone."

They kissed for a long time and then he held her close. "You're the most important person in the world to me," he whispered and kissed her again. In a few minutes, she settled against him, held tightly in his embrace.

"Boone, I need to go call the insurance adjuster."

He kissed her temple. "I suppose you're right." He rolled away and leaned down to look at her. "When things settle tonight, let's still go to dinner. I want to talk about our future."

Her pulse jumped as she nodded and watched him walk away.

In minutes he emerged from the bathroom in his wet jeans, pulling on his boots.

"What are you doing?" she asked.

"I better see if the men need help and if everyone is all right."

She sat up and swung her legs out of bed. "I'll come with you."

"No you don't," he said firmly. "You're staying right here—high and dry. I'll report back and I'll call if you're needed, but I can tell you now that you won't be. There wasn't one man out there who wanted you to be there."

"Men!" she snapped in disgust. "I got several horses out of there."

"So you did," he said grimly. "Now, you stay put."

"Yes, sir," she said in a sarcastic voice, and he grinned.

"See you soon," he said, and was gone.

She got out of bed and got a robe, pulling it on and going to a window where she could see the stables and see what was happening.

The rain had stopped and a rainbow arced across the sky. The blackened ruins still smoldered and small columns of gray smoke rose in the air. Men milled about and the corral held restless horses.

If no horses or men had been injured or lost, they were indeed fortunate, and she realized that she should have listened more closely to Boone about building new stables, particularly when the fire chief agreed with him.

Was she also turning a deaf ear to him about his feelings on getting married? she wondered. She knew he had meant his declaration of love this afternoon. The words hadn't been said out of any sense of duty.

Today he had acted like a man who was in love. She watched Boone cross the yard and join the other men. Perry joined him and the two men talked. She moved away to go to her office and call the insurance adjuster and tell him about the blaze.

When she had finished talking to him, she showered again. In spite of Boone's urging her to stay home, she was going to go see the damage for herself.

When she stepped out of the shower, the phone was ringing and she picked up the receiver to hear Boone's voice.

"Darlin', I miss you."

She laughed. "You just left me, Boone. What about the men? Was anyone hurt?"

"Nope. Only scratches and minor burns. Everyone is all right, and all the horses are okay."

"Thank heavens!" she exclaimed in relief. "I talked to the adjuster and he's coming out. I just showered and I don't have on a stitch—"

"Erin," Boone said in a low voice. "I'll be right there."

She laughed. "No, you stay and do what you have to do."

"I don't suppose you'd just wait there in the shower for me?"

"Bye, Boone," she said with a smile, and hung up the phone.

She dressed in cutoffs and a T-shirt, pulling on sneakers.

She caught her hair up in a clip and then went downstairs to walk to the ruins.

Boone was talking to a fireman and saw her coming. He left the fireman and came to meet her.

"You didn't pay any attention to me asking you to stay home."

"No. The adjuster is on his way here—"

"He's already been here and I've talked to him."

"That was quick."

"Yes, it was. He'll get back to us in the morning. The firemen will hang around tonight to make sure no sparks flare up. There goes the evening we'd planned. How about just coming to my place to eat?"

"That's fine with me," she replied as she stood looking at the ashes and charred boards. She shivered. "Boone, I should have listened. This could have been dreadful."

He squeezed her shoulders. "Don't worry about it. The stable is gone and no one was badly injured, no horses lost. Now we can get rid of another one and build two new stables."

"Get rid of all three of them. I don't want to look at any of them because I'll always remember trying to get those horses and myself out of the fire."

"Good. I'm glad to hear you say that. I've already called a firm to come out and give us some estimates."

She looked up at him. "Boone, the fences can be replaced, too. I've hung on to the old ways when I shouldn't have."

"Stop worrying," he said. "We can discuss all that later. The big thing is that you and our baby are safe. "

He hugged her lightly and she buried her face against his chest. He smelled of smoke, but she didn't care. *Our baby.* His words warmed her heart.

"I see your uncle and one of the firemen looking at us, Erin," Boone said, releasing her.

"I better see if Uncle Perry wants to talk to me," she said.

"I'll check with them. You go home. If they need you, I'll come get you."

When she walked to her house, Boone called, "How about half past seven?"

She nodded and turned away. Still shaken by the fire, she knew she would never forget it. Nor would she forget how stubbornly she had clung to old ways.

At a quarter before seven, dressed in black silk slacks with a black silk halter top and her hair looped and pinned on her head, Erin walked to Boone's house and entered through one of the back doors. "Boone?" she called to him.

He came out of the kitchen and smiled at her, and her heartbeat quickened. He was in a brown shirt and slacks and looked marvelous.

"Hi, beautiful lady," he said, walking up and sweeping her into his arms to lean over her and kiss her soundly. He swung her upright again and released her. "Do you look gorgeous!"

She smiled at him. "Thank you. You look rather great yourself."

"Come have a glass of ice water or whatever you're allowed to drink now."

"Ice water sounds fine," she answered. And he laced his fingers through hers to hold her hand as they went to the kitchen.

They sat on the terrace where he had a table set with a white linen cloth. They ate a tossed salad and then Boone grilled steaks and had twice-baked potatoes and steamed asparagus. The dinner was delicious, but she could barely eat because all her attention was on Boone.

The sun slowly set and lights came on at the fringe of the terrace. Boone lit the candle in the center of their table and he had soft music playing. A cool breeze made the setting perfect and she forgot the afternoon's crisis, her worries and problems, just relishing being with Boone.

They both left half-eaten dinners while they talked and he made her laugh. She felt giddy, happy, still wondering if he really knew his own feelings.

It was almost dark beyond the terrace when Boone pushed away his chair and took her hand to pull her up into his arms.

She thought he was going to dance, but instead, he held her lightly with his arms around her waist. He gazed down at her solemnly and then framed her face with his hands.

"Erin, I love you with all my being," he said in a rush, and her heart thudded. "I want you to marry me. I'm not asking out of duty or obligation or any of those reasons. When I told you that I would never marry, I didn't know what it meant to really be in love with someone. I've had affairs, but I've never been deeply in love."

She gazed into his eyes, held totally by his solemn words and expression.

"Erin, I'm in love. I love you and I don't want to be away from you or live without you."

"Oh, Boone!" she whispered, tightening her fingers around his while her heart thudded. "And you really want this baby? You said you'd had all the diapers and bottles—"

"Erin, those were brothers and sisters. That is entirely different. Yes, I want our baby! I want you to be my wife."

"You've been so sure most of your life that you didn't want to marry," she said quietly.

"I told you, I've never been in love before. Erin, everything you do is special to me," he said in a husky voice. "I think about you all the time and I want you more every day we're together. I want you to be my wife. I want to come home to you, have this baby with you. I will love you forever."

"You're not doing this because I'm pregnant? I want the truth," she said.

"I swear, I'm not. If you found out tomorrow that you aren't really pregnant, I'd still propose to you. I've thought about it and I hate being away from you. And I couldn't bear it when you said you wanted us to stop seeing each other. You're special, Erin. So incredibly special. I love you," he said. "Will you marry me?"

She closed her eyes as joy made her shake.

"Ah, Erin, I know how I feel and what I want," he continued, and she realized he thought she didn't believe him. Her eyes flew open and she flung her arms around his neck.

"Yes! Oh, yes! I love you with all my heart!"

His arms tightened around her instantly and he leaned down to kiss her, holding her close in his embrace.

When he drew away, she looked into his blue eyes and saw the love shining in them. Holding her with one arm, he fished in his pocket and withdrew a small black box to hold out to her.

Wordlessly, with trembling fingers, she opened it and looked at a dazzling diamond. "Oh, Boone!"

"It's just a token of my love, a way to bind you to me forever, darlin'."

She threw her arms around his neck again and kissed him long and hard. The next time he stopped her, his eyes had darkened with passion. He swept her into his arms and carried her inside to a bedroom to make love to her.

"I do mean it, and you said yes." He picked up the ring to slide it on her finger. Then he kissed her, and Erin forgot where they were and everything else except the tall man holding her in his arms and declaring his love for her.

Later, when she was wrapped in his arms in bed, he lay propped on his elbow and looked down at her.

"Erin, let's not wait long for this wedding. I'm talking about this week or next."

"You have a huge family. I want to meet each one of them and I want you to meet my sister and you're not rushing me into a wedding."

"Don't take months. I can't stand that."

"Not months, but more than days!" she replied, laughing. Happiness welled up in her, making her giddy. She was marrying Boone!

"Darlin', you've made me the happiest man on earth tonight," he said in a husky voice that sent a thrill spiraling through her.

She placed her hand on his cheek. "I love you. And I hope you mean what you say in the depths of your heart."

"I do. I know what I want. It's you, darlin'. That was pure hell being without you. How soon can we have a wedding?"

"How about two months from today?"

"How about one month from today?"

She laughed. "All right, but you'd better help me with everything!" She stroked his cheek. "Are you going to get your way all our married lives?"

"I'm going to try, but my main aim is to please you—is one month so bad?"

"No, it's not bad," she said, smiling at him. "It's not bad at all." She looked at her sparkling new diamond ring and knew that the next month would fly past as if it were only a day. She tightened her arm around Boone's neck and pulled his head closer so she could kiss him again.

Epilogue

It was the first weekend in October with bright sunshine and blue skies on a Saturday morning. Erin could not believe that her wedding day was finally here. They had settled on the first week in October, slightly longer than Boone wanted, but not a lot longer.

She sat still while her sister, Mary, straightened her veil.

"You look beautiful," Tina Courtland said, and Erin smiled at her friend.

"My baby and I, you mean," Erin said, patting her stomach and smiling.

"You hardly even show," Mary said.

"My waist is thicker, but that's all right," Erin replied.

"You look absolutely gorgeous," Mary Frye agreed. "And you're marrying someone so handsome that I can't believe he's not in movies. What a waste! Sure you don't want to come out to California and let your husband get into movies?"

"I'm sure," Erin replied with amusement, looking at her

image in the mirror. At Boone's request, she wore the ancient necklace, the emerald cross on the heavy gold chain. Her white silk wedding gown was total simplicity with thin straps and a straight neckline and slim skirt with a long, removable train.

Her hair was piled on her head with some tendrils curling around her face, and her veil was turned back, forming a gauzy halo around her face.

Her sister stood close beside her and they looked at each other in the mirror. Older, slightly taller, Mary's brunette hair was a dark contrast to Erin's red hair. Mary smiled at her sister and squeezed her waist. "I'm so happy for you." She dabbed at tears that came to her eyes.

"Mary, don't cry!" Erin exclaimed. "I'm happy. It's all wonderful. Boone is marvelous and our baby is wonderful."

"I know. I'm just happy for you."

Wanting to get the wedding started and over, wanting to be Mrs. Boone Devlin, Erin glanced at the clock.

"It's time," Tina said, looking at the clock, too. Mary handed Erin her bouquet of white orchids, tulips and roses and Erin turned to go, stepping into the church hall.

Her uncle was escorting her down the aisle, and when she met him, he wiped tears from his eyes.

"How I wish your daddy could see you. You're beautiful, Erin, and he would be so proud of you. Your daddy and your mama both."

She patted Perry's hand that was on her arm. "I'm glad you're here to walk me down the aisle. That would please Dad."

Perry nodded, and then they went to the foyer and waited while Mary walked down the aisle and then Tina and another friend, Gracie.

At last it was time for Erin and she took a deep breath and

walked beside her uncle. The moment she turned through the wide doorway, she saw the crowded sanctuary, the wedding party, and then her gaze flew to meet Boone's.

He was more handsome than ever in a tux that heightened his dashing dark looks. Tall, standing straight, he was watching her and the rest of the church and guests vanished from her consciousness. She couldn't hear the music for her pounding heart. She was marrying the love of her life! Joy overwhelmed her and she couldn't stop smiling.

Boone stood waiting, looking at Erin walk down the aisle and he was dazzled by her beauty, thinking he was marrying the most beautiful woman in the world.

He was awed, feeling incredibly lucky, frightened when he thought how close he had come to losing her through his own foolishness. How could he have ever wanted to say no to marriage to Erin? And she was having their baby!

This was all better than that fabulous inheritance he had received from John Frates and if he had to choose one or the other, he would pick marriage to Erin without hesitation.

Then she was right there, gazing up at him and he was dazzled, trembling with excitement and feeling like the luckiest man on earth. He took her hand and they repeated vows that he never even heard and finally he could kiss the bride. His bride. Erin Devlin. It was magic. He kissed her lightly, feeling her warm soft lips beneath his.

"Forever, darlin'," he whispered in her ear and then he straightened and wrapped her arm in his. They walked back up the aisle as man and wife.

The celebration began when they reached the foyer. Boone swept her into his arms and spun around.

"Boone!" she cried, laughing with him. "Put me down! We have to do pictures!"

"Love you, Mrs. Devlin."

"And I love you. Are you sober?"

"Haven't touched a drop of alcohol, but sober? No. I'm overjoyed and can't hold it in."

"Well, hang on for a couple more hours," she said. "Now put me down and let's get the picture-taking over with."

They posed for pictures and then were driven in a white limousine to the Stallion Pass Country Club for the wedding reception that spread from the ballroom across the terrace. A band played and Erin danced the first dance in her new husband's arms, looking up at him and knowing she would remember this moment for the rest of her life.

"I love you, Mrs. Devlin, and can't believe that you're mine."

"That I am, Boone," she said solemnly. "I love you beyond measure. You are the only man I've ever loved."

"And you, darlin', are definitely the only woman I've loved. Erin, you're so incredibly special."

"You've made me so happy," she whispered, dancing in his arms and enveloped in love, looking up at his thick brown hair and deep blue eyes and wondering how such a handsome man had fallen in love with her.

"How long do we have to do this?" he asked.

"About another hour and then maybe we can slip away."

"I'll work on that. You schmooze the crowd, and in an hour I'll come get you."

"If you get to enjoying yourself and want to stay, we can," Erin said.

"You don't want to be with me?"

"Of course I want to be with you! More than you can imagine."

"Don't think so, darlin'," he drawled, wrapping his arms around her and dancing close.

"Boone, everyone is watching us. Behave."

"I'm a man in love."

She smiled and danced with him and then with Uncle Perry. Next, several of the Double T cowboys took turns dancing with her and wishing her well.

Later, after the cake had been cut, Boone was standing with a group of friends. Mike Remington wished him well and Jonah Whitewolf looked at him with a twinkle in his eye.

"I think it's time we passed that white stallion on to the new husband. So your wedding present from me will be delivered in about a week."

"What white stallion?" Boone asked, and then remembered the legend and that one of the men had given the horse to Jonah when he married. He looked around the circle of men and realized they had gotten together about this. "All you guys have owned this horse, haven't you?" he asked, looking at Gabriel Brant, Josh Kellogg and Wyatt Sawyer, men who had grown up in the area.

"That's right," Mike said. "Then Wyatt gave him to me and I passed him on to Jonah. He's getting to be our wedding gift horse."

"Not a white elephant, but a white stallion," Jonah said, and the others laughed.

"Gabe, Josh, Wyatt, Mike and now Jonah—that horse is going to wear away from being passed from person to person," Boone said. "And I hate to look a gift horse in the mouth, but we have a lot of horses and I think my wife is rather particular about bloodlines."

"You can keep him off to himself," Mike said, grinning. "We don't want to break the chain."

"Erin has her own tie to that legend. She's supposed to be related to the woman who lost her love, the brave warrior."

"All the more reason you should have the horse," Jonah said. He clapped Boone on the back. "That horse is yours. Of course, he's not exactly wild any longer. Wyatt tamed him."

"And then, Jonah has never seen a horse he couldn't ride," Mike said dryly, "so he's a little on the tame side now, but we've got to keep the legend going and at the same time ensure that you find your true love."

"I found her and I don't need the help of you guys or your white horse."

"We'll have a barbecue at our place and celebrate when Jonah delivers the horse," Gabe Brant said.

"Maybe we should have the barbecue at his place," Mike suggested, "so we can watch him ride the stallion."

"I'm not riding that horse for the benefit of you guys. Besides, I've had my rounds with one of Erin's, an old roan that will make your white horse look like a gentle lamb."

"Hey, let's have a contest," Wyatt said. "You ride the white stallion, and I'll ride your roan."

"I'll take you up on that one," Boone said, laughing with them.

"Here comes your wife to rescue you," Mike said. "I heard she rescued you from Perry and the boys. Looks like all that army training just couldn't stand up against a bunch of Texas cowboys."

"Yeah," Jonah teased. "I heard you had bruised ribs and black eyes—"

"You guys," Boone said, and turned to smile at Erin and slip his arm around her waist. "Let's get out of here, darlin'. I've had enough of these locals yahoos with their horse tales and conniving plans."

"Conniving plans?" she asked, looking at his grinning friends.

"That's right. Come on. See you guys later. A whole hell of a lot later. Like in a couple of months." He led her away and she looked up at him.

"What was all that about?"

"I'll tell you, but first you tell me—it's been two hours. How much longer before we can split?"

"How about right now?" she asked. "Unless you want—"

Boone's arm tightened around her waist and he rushed through the nearest door and closed it before she could finish her sentence.

"I have a getaway car waiting that no one—absolutely no one except me—knows about. C'mon, Mrs. Devlin. Let's go!"

As the first rays of sun came over the horizon and waves lapped gently along the beach, Erin lay in Boone's arms in the bedroom of the villa on their own tropical island. Boone had leased the island for the month and it was their second morning before she remembered Boone's conversation with his friends. She raised up on one elbow and trailed her fingers over Boone's bare chest.

"What was all that about when you talked about getting away from your conniving friends?"

Boone reached over to pick up the cross necklace that was on the table beside the bed. Light caught in the depths of emeralds and gave back green fire. "This reminds me of your eyes and it reminds me of the first night I met you," he said in a husky voice. He put the cross back on the table and played with locks of Erin's hair.

"Those guys are passing that damn white stallion on to me to keep the legend going of someone finding true love if they have that horse."

She laughed. "That's ridiculous! We don't need that stallion at our place, but if they said they're going to do that, if Wyatt Sawyer and Josh are involved, I know they'll do what they say. I don't know your friends that well, but I know Gabe and Wyatt and Josh. We're not keeping that horse, though. I don't want any wild bloodlines getting mixed in with our fine horses."

"You may have a wild bloodline mixed in with your fine Frye family," he said, grinning.

"That one I'll put up with," she said, nuzzling his neck.

"The guys are going to have a barbecue—actually, it might be at our place. Wyatt and I have a little bet, but nothing placed on the outcome yet. They're probably taking wagers now."

"What kind of wager?" she asked, drawing a circle on his shoulder with her tongue. His skin tasted salty and she knew it was from the sweat that had popped out on him earlier when they had been making love.

"He's going to ride Tornado and I'm going to ride the white stallion. Winner is the one who stays on the longest."

"Why would you get yourself into something like that?" she asked, sitting up and frowning, pulling the sheet up beneath her arms.

"It'll be worth it to watch Tornado throw Wyatt into the next county. 'Course, from what I've heard, Wyatt Sawyer must be a damn fine rider. But the roan is cussed and he'll toss Wyatt, or my name isn't Boone Devlin." Boone reached up to trail his fingers along the top of the sheet, following her curves.

"Come here, Mrs. Devlin. I can't say that enough or kiss you enough or love you enough."

She wrapped her arms around his neck and slid down in bed against him, turning her face up as she pulled him closer to kiss him. Her heart pounded with joy and she leaned back. "Boone, I love you and you've made me happy beyond my wildest imaginings or longings. You and our baby—how could I want anything else in life?"

"You will, sweetie," he said, trailing kisses along her

cheek. "I'll wager you'll want this baby to have a little brother or sister someday."

She kissed Boone lightly. "You're absolutely right," she whispered, and then tightened her arms to kiss him, joy brimming over in her because she was wildly in love and she expected to stay that way far, far into the future.

* * * * *

Everyone thought Colin Garrick was dead...
But this fourth Texan Knight is undoubtedly alive, and he's come to Stallion Pass with a mission...and a warning.
Colin had closed off his wounded heart long ago, but when a spunky nanny gets caught in the middle of his plans and sets sparks of passion flying between them, he'll do anything in his power to protect her!

Sara's tantalizing tales of these Texas Knights continue in
Silhouette Intimate Moments
with
DON'T CLOSE YOUR EYES
Coming in September 2004
only from Silhouette Books

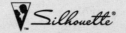

From bestselling author

BEVERLY BARTON

Laying His Claim
(Silhouette Desire #1598)

After Kate and Trent Winston's daughter was kidnapped, their marriage collapsed from the trauma. Ten years later, Kate discovers that their daughter might still be alive. Amidst their intense search, Kate and Trent find something else they'd lost: hot, passionate sexual chemistry. Now, can they claim the happy ending they deserve?

**Ready to lay their lives on the line,
but unprepared for the power of love!**

Available August 2004 at your favorite retail outlet.

COMING NEXT MONTH

#1597 STEAMY SAVANNAH NIGHTS—Sheri WhiteFeather
Dynasties: The Danforths
Bodyguard Michael Whittaker was intensely drawn to illegitimate
Danforth daughter Lea Nguyen. He knew she was keeping secrets
and Michael's paid pursuit soon spilled into voluntary overtime. They
couldn't resist the Savannah heat that burned between them, yet could
they withstand the forces that were against them?

#1598 LAYING HIS CLAIM—Beverly Barton
The Protectors
After Kate and Trent Winston's daughter was kidnapped, their marriage
collapsed from the trauma. Ten years later, Kate discovered that their
daughter might still be alive. Amidst their intense search, Kate and Trent
found something else they'd lost: hot, passionate sexual chemistry. Now,
could they claim the happy ending they deserved?

#1599 BETWEEN DUTY AND DESIRE—Leanne Banks
Mantalk
A promise to a fallen comrade had brought marine corporal
Brock Armstrong to Callie Newton's home. He'd vowed to help the
widow move on with her life, but he'd had no idea Callie would call
to him so deeply, placing Brock in the tense position between duty and
desire.

#1600 PERSUADING THE PLAYBOY KING—Kristi Gold
The Royal Wager
Playboy prince Marcel Frederic DeLoria bet his Harvard buddies
that he'd still be unattached by their tenth reunion. But when he was
unexpectedly crowned, the sweet and sexy Kate Milner entered his
kingdom. Could Kate persuade this playboy king to lose his royal wager?

#1601 STONE COLD SURRENDER—Brenda Jackson
Madison Winters was never one for a quick fling, but when she met
sexy Stone Westmoreland, the bestselling author taught the proper
schoolteacher a lesson worth learning: when it came to passion, even
the most sensible soul could lose their sensibilities.

#1602 AWAKEN TO PLEASURE—Nalini Singh
Stunningly sexy Jackson Santorini couldn't wait to call a one-on-one
conference with his former secretary, Taylor Reid. But—despite his
tender touch—Taylor was tentative to enter into a romantic liaison.
Could Jackson seduce the bedroom-shy Taylor and successfully awaken
her to pleasure?

SDCNM0704